"Such a strong first impression—haunting in the best way."

ALIX E. HARROW
of *The Ten Thousand Doors of January*

"A haunting, genre-defying novel that blends magical realism, and a modern exploration of family, trauma, and the supernatural. It's a deeply layered, poetic, and unsettling work that plays with themes of faith, belief, and the search for connection in a fractured world."

JOSE CARDEIRO, author of *The Death of Death*, a global bestseller

"A raw and edgy book that reads like the love child of Kathy Acker and Elmore Leonard. Ayla's voice spins a kind of confessionalist noir as she leads us down a twisty rabbit hole of memory, loss, and imagination, poetically blurring all three."

MICHAEL HARRIS COHEN, author of *The Eyes*

"From the amnesiac hospital room to the swamp symbolizing the dark recesses of trauma, Ayla searches for her missing sister in a world where memories are entombed as deeply as secrets. And even if some stories are better left buried, the novel—in more than one respect—is utterly unflinching."

ANGEL IGOV, author of *A Short Tale of Shame*

"Beneath the swamp's still surface, a secret stirs.

Nectar is a gripping page-turner that pulls you in from the first page and never lets go. Each chapter unveils new clues and dark secrets, stoking your curiosity and keeping you guessing long into the night.

The final revelation is a gut-punch twist that flips the whole story on its head. Bold and unflinching, this novel feels destined for literary success."

IORDAN MATEEV, Publisher of *Forbes Bulgaria*

NECTAR

Kanina Krisalis

NECTAR

Sounds of Soft Things Breaking

a novel

Sofia, 2025

This novel is a work of fiction. Names, characters, places and incidents are either the product of the author's imagination or are used fictitiously. Any resemblance to actual persons, living or dead, events or locales, is entirely coincidental.

All rights reserved. No part of this publication may be reproduced, transmitted, or stored in a retrieval system, in any form or by any means, electronic, mechanical, photocopying, recording or otherwise, without the prior permission of the author.

NECTAR. SOUNDS OF SOFT THINGS BREAKING
Kanina Krisalis
First edition, 2025

© Kanina Krisalis, author, 2025
© Fabian Aerts, cover design, 2025
© Fabian Aerts, cover illustration, 2025
© Fabian Aerts, illustration, 2025
© Emil Markov, for the illustration, page 134, 2025

© Locus Publishing, Ltd., 2025
INK is a trademark of Locus Publishing

ISBN: 979-828-223-334-6

For Stoyan
For Papo
For my sister(s)

01: COMA

"What a way to die. And so young."

"She's not dead," someone—a man—said.

"Looks pretty dead to me."

"Not yet." His voice clipped, steady. And I'd try to remember that voice. I'd hold on to it. Like a tick latching onto flesh.

The flashlight fried my eyeballs. "Stop that," I commanded, but no words came out. The person cracked open my left eye. Something small and round floated in a milky whiteness. A button. A white button over a spotless uniform. The figure smelled faintly of fresh soap. God, my clothes could never be that neat. As pristine as a freshly made sheet of paper.

The harsh glare of his flashlight came for me again. "I said, stop that." Again, nothing, zero, nada.

Some years ago, still in Thessaloniki, some guy with a huge camera pointed it at my face and started shooting—bam, bam, bam—twenty, maybe thirty shots in rapid succession. It was the same unsanitary sensation. He wanted to take the perfect photo of my irises and create a digital painting. He used the word *art*.

The man looked into my eyes—one blue, the other a restless mix of blue and brown. "That's something rare," he said. His long ponytail clung to the back of his neck, matted with sweat. A slick shine glazed his balding forehead, slipping and shifting like oil whenever he moved.

He steadied my face, thumb pressing below my eye, index finger above, stretching the lid wide open until my eye threatened to pop. "Stay still," he commanded, while the camera pulsed with light. My vision blurred for a second, but I held it, just long enough for him to get what he needed.

"Again," he muttered.

It was all kinds of disgusting—the person, the feeling, the way he touched my temples. And my eyes felt the same way they did that day. What surprised me was how lovely the final photograph came out, pruned of any of that.

I'd been asked something.

"Disoriented to time, place and person," someone said.

He was right, the man who said that. Disoriented to my own person; no bullshit there. Guilty as charged. And my parents knew that all too well. I had the idea to count all the lies I'd ever told them, but they were more numerous than my days. Not interested. Bye-bye now.

I had one hundred cats nesting on my head and body. They all purred and rubbed against me and one another, and their fur funneled through my mouth and nostrils, filling my lungs, liver, heart. It was suffocating and oddly comforting, as though I was being consumed by softness.

Today, some cats had left.

Today, all the cats became one big rotting animal nestling inside my mouth. There was no air—just a taste of shit, and a sponge for a tongue. I wanted to open my mouth for that stench to come out. I commanded it to open. And, again, it wouldn't. And then, in that suffocating stillness, I dreamed of my mother, handing me my toothbrush, the bristles smeared with sweet strawberry paste.

A hand—someone's, I never saw who—pressed a toothbrush between my lips and brushed gently, like they knew how much I craved it. *I don't know who you are, but I love you.* The mint flooded my mouth, cooling the rotten surface, sowing green seeds of freshness where decay had made its home. I drifted in the sensation, weightless, as if floating between two worlds. I tried to focus, to commit the moment to memory—this small kindness, this reprieve from the stale bitterness of my unconscious self.

I woke up to what could be the next morning or next week, but with a companion in my bed. His name was Pain. He was a hulking, dark brute who wanted revenge for all the injustice in the world. And he delivered it to me, ramming his huge cock deep into my urethra.

"Her catheter is displaced," some woman said.

That ought to be my punishment for being a bitch to so many people.

I cried out from the pain before I even knew I was awake, before I saw anything at all.

My body throbbed as if it had never belonged to me. The air felt dense and wrong. Then I opened my eyes, and there was my father. Next to him, a label taped on the machine, which flickered in and out of focus: Ayla, 22.

My father moved closer to the bed, hesitant, like he was afraid of touching something fragile. And then he cried, his breath catching in short, shuddering gasps. His shoulders sagged, as if he were a child who'd done something terrible. I couldn't look away from him. I was astonished and horrified. For some reason, this mattered to me. I don't know why. But it did.

I tried to speak, but my throat was dry and raw.

"Where the fuck am I?" I finally asked.

"In the hospital, Ayla." His words trembled, barely holding their shape.

What grabbed my attention was my own hand. It was completely bruised, hooked up to an IV. That was when I realized there were tubes coming out of my body—five in total.

"Saint Luke's Hospital," my father added. "You were in an accident, and you've been here a week." His words landed like stones. His voice always had weight, but now it sagged under the burden of saying something heavier.

I was just so tired.

"Ayla," he said, "do you... do you know where Selen is?"

"Selen?" I repeated, the name tumbling out of my mouth. "Who's that?" My mind shuffled through its files, but there was nothing there. "Why are tubes sticking out of me?"

The way he recoiled—it wasn't just hurt. His face hardened, a crack forming in the mask he usually wore around me. The shift was instant.

"Don't," my father said, low and cold.

"Don't what?"

"Don't pretend you don't know who I'm speaking of!"

I stared at him. The name floated somewhere above me, like a big bird circling, never coming down.

"Now is not the time for your little games. We only have a minute," my dad hissed, his voice sharpening. "Was Selen with you that night? What happened to her?"

"I don't know what you're talking about," I snapped, breaking against the weight of his anger. My head pounded, a stabbing pain radiating out from my temple, and, for a moment, I thought I might throw up. I tried to push myself up, but the cast and tubes pinned me to the bed.

"You're lying even now," he said. Not a question. A statement. He leaned closer, his jaw tight. "Where is she?"

"Tell the doctor to give me painkillers and leave, Father. I'm in pain."

The room fell into a tense, awful silence. My father straightened, his mouth a thin, bloodless line, his nostrils flaring in a silent accusation.

The beeping of the monitor filled the space, echoing the wild thrum of my pulse.

"Will you leave already?" I asked my father. He muttered something under his breath, and then finally left.

When I was little, not more than six, and angry at my father, I'd storm out of the room, slam the door behind me, and shout, "Leave! Get out! I hate you!" Then I'd collapse onto my bed and cry—loudly, theatrically—hoping he'd hear me. But even as I screamed, I was always listening, straining for the sound of his footsteps. I ached for him to appear in the doorway, even though my mouth would insist he leave me alone. And it made me so happy when he didn't listen. I told him to go, but more than anything, I wanted him to stay.

"Your injuries are incompatible with you being alive," the doctor explained. Well, lucky me. They had just moved me to the pulmonary ward from the Intensive Care Unit;

wheeled me in like baggage. There was something detached in his voice—not cruelty, but weariness. As if he'd tried to be compassionate once, long ago, and had given up. Three days they'd kept me in an induced coma. Three days they'd kept me under, leaving me in that liminal space between here and not here. His voice was still hanging there in the air, but I wasn't sure if he was waiting for me to speak.

"The body's resilient—it adapts. But it doesn't happen overnight." He stood there, tall, angular, with purple hollows beneath his eyes that screamed *I haven't slept in days, but I'm not about to whine about it.* He didn't look at me. He looked at the chart.

There was something distant and untouchable about the doctor. He could probably look at a mangled corpse and not flinch. But I felt warmth toward him anyway. A creeping desire—not to be pitied, not to be saved, but to please him somehow, to earn his approval, to show him I wasn't like the others he saw in this place; crumpled bodies discarded in hospital beds. I was different, or I could be, if he would just notice. That thought, shameful and absurd, burned in me as I lay there, unable to move, my body reduced to a fragile weight beneath the sheets.

"You are in recovery from multiple surgeries," the doctor added. "The drains in your lower abdomen collect any residual blood and fluid from the procedures. Three drains on the side of your chest are helping to remove excess fluid from your lungs. That's standard after trauma like yours."

"And that?" I asked, pointing weakly at the bandage wrapped tight across my chest.

The doctor didn't even blink. "That's where we opened you up."

He glanced at the monitors, then back at me. "We'll monitor you closely. You're in good hands."

I stared at him, waiting for more—for the part that explained why this happened, what exactly *this* was. But he just folded his hands, his gaze hovering somewhere between me and the door. He seemed utterly pained for having to explain anything medical to me.

Days bled into each other; nights stretched long, pulled thin like an unraveling thread. Yet waking up carried the cruelest trick—an instant of weightless peace before reality settled in. For a second, you were fine. The pain hadn't arrived yet. And then it crashed over you with force, unstoppable and absolute.

Unbreak me, Mr. Doctor.

Lying in that bed ate me alive. The sheets held me too tightly, the mattress absorbing my shape. It wasn't just where I was—it became who I was. My mouth tasted metallic, as if I had been swallowing rust. I needed an escape, something to pry me out of myself—a book, a movie, anything to force me into a different shape. A coming-of-age story about a wild girl. Life had kicked her, so she kicked back. The kind where she was good at heart, where people pulled her into their arms and held her at the end. Sometimes, the heroine even developed a superpower.

I also had a special power. To fuck up everything I touched. And the only thing holding me now was the plaster cast clinging to my broken leg. I often wanted to be other people, and now the need was eating at me, stronger than anything and everything. It was a matter of survival. A daydream carried me to the forest, where I ran among the trees.

I filled the bag with urine. Pissing stung. But the first shit post-accident was an ordeal all its own. I was immobilized, flat on my back, reliant on nurses and bedpans. The meds, the fucking trauma—everything clogged my system. It took days, sometimes even a week, before my bowels stirred again. And when they did, the cramps came first, rolling through my gut like cleavers.

An event like this—a car wreck—was supposed to change something within me. Open up a hidden chamber in my soul, some divine wisdom. That didn't happen. I just wanted to be out of here, for the pain to stop, for the dull, insistent misery to let go. My desires were so simple, so basic. Stop the pain. Stop the boredom. No revelations, no grand insight. Just the wish to return to the same life I'd almost destroyed trying to escape.

I couldn't remember the accident from beginning to end. They said it was a car accident. And sure, it made sense—what else? I remembered the club. The music was loud. I was dancing, leaning into strangers like they could hold me up. Drinking. Kissing somebody—maybe more than one somebody. Pills, too. Whatever they handed me. I didn't ask what it was. Just swallowed it down with the burn of cheap vodka and kept going. The night was spinning, unraveling, but I remembered getting in the car.

My mother, when she came to visit with my father, kept asking about this girl—Selen— she said, like I was supposed to know. Did something happen to her?

"Did I kill someone?" I asked my mother.

Her face didn't change at first, not really. A flicker of something crossed her eyes—there, then gone. "No, darling," she said finally. "Why are you saying this? Is there anything else you remember?"

I shook my head. My throat felt dry. "Where's my phone?"

"You no longer have a phone. The police took it as evidence."

"As evidence?"

She nodded, her hands clasped tightly in her lap. "Yes. They're still investigating. It's standard procedure."

"When will they return it?" I asked her. That phone was the natural extension of my arm.

"Ayla...," she hesitated, then sighed. "I don't think they will."

My parents tried to appear calm, but their soft, worried eyes betrayed their unease.

"What becomes of those without money or means?" my father suddenly asked, breaking his silence.

I blinked at him. For a second, I was relieved, grateful for the distraction. A hundred thousand euros—that was what my stay here was going to cost. Just the hospital. Not the months of rehabilitation. A hundred thousand euros. It sounded like a fake number.

"I guess they just die," I said.

"Ayla, listen. I'll pay for everything. Whatever you need. I'll pay your college tuition so you can graduate. But this is it... it's the last I can do for you. I can't keep doing this. There'll be no apartment. And if I hear you've been drinking or taking stuff again... that's it. Something has to change."

What did you think was going to change, Father? Me?

My father had arrived in Thessaloniki as the Turkish Consul General, expecting to stay a few years, maybe five at most. That was how it worked—diplomats came and went, their lives packed neatly into trunks and crates, their names fading from memory before the ink on the next appointment letter had dried. Cities did not belong to them, and they did not belong to cities. But my father never believed in such arrangements. He had a way of settling into places, of making himself necessary, until people stopped remembering a time before he was there.

At first, it must have been just small things: the way he learned the rhythm of the city, the particular slowness of mornings by the port, the bakery owner who began setting aside a warm koulouri for him without asking. A name called out from a market stall. A nod from a tailor who had adjusted his suits more times than either of them could count. And then, at some point, he must have realized he wasn't leaving.

The house in Panorama came later, when leaving was no longer a question but a forgotten possibility. It stood high above the city, solid and immovable, as if it had been there long before him, waiting. Stone by stone, it rooted him deeper into Thessaloniki, its wide balconies opening to the sea, its foundations gripping the hillside, saying: *This is home now.*

He was in love with the city. I honestly think one of the reasons he married my mother was because she had lived here her whole life. More Greek than him, she taught him how to blend in, how to walk through Thessaloniki like he had always belonged. And he learned quickly. His Turkishness softened, settled, until no one could quite say where he was from. Walking the streets of Thessaloniki, you felt like you were treading on the remains of something ancient, yet alive in the cracks of the stones. Maybe this was what he loved most—the feeling that the past could live alongside him, that he could thread himself into its story.

Fourteen years passed. Longer than any consul should stay, but no one ever questioned it. By then, Thessaloniki had grown into my father, filling the spaces in him that might have once belonged to somewhere else. He had made himself indispensable, woven so deeply into the city's affairs that removing him would have left a gap no one knew quite how to fill. When his official post ended, he remained, though the title was different now, something quieter, more elusive. "Call it diplomacy, call it counsel," he would say, a faint smile playing at the edge of his mouth. "People still come to me when they need something done."

He walked the streets as if he had poured the concrete himself, his steps measured, deliberate, as if Thessaloniki followed his rhythm. "The architect of countless trade agreements and whispered negotiations," he liked to recite, though what he really meant was, *I matter here.*

My father could command a room without trying. People, silence, even the goddamn air. Me? I could barely command my own shadow. To him, I wasn't a daughter; I was a mistake. A smudge on his perfect blueprint. Proof that, for all his precision, something in his grand design had gone horribly wrong.

My face felt wrong—swollen, sunken, ugly in a way that didn't make sense; like I wasn't wearing it right. My hair had turned into a wild, knotted mess, something you couldn't comb through without pulling out half of it. I didn't have anything to say to anyone. So I stayed here, silent, waiting. Letting two weeks crawl by like they weren't mine to live, just something to sit through until I could leave myself behind.

Every morning, the doctors came for rounds, checked my temperature, and inspected the drains. Every other day, they wheeled me off for X-rays to monitor my lungs. My breathing was still shallow, as if my body had forgotten how to take in more air.

At first, I couldn't get out of bed. Everything from my body drained into bags, catheters, and bedpans. No movement. Just lying on my back. My tasks were almost laughable—blowing into a bottle through a straw to train my lungs, and inflating balloons.

At 8 a.m., the doctor would come. He'd glance at my chart, barely at me, then speak to the nurse outside, as if they shared a secret I wasn't allowed to hear. But I waited for him. Even that distant attention was something to hold on to. Maybe this was what Stockholm syndrome felt like.

At 9 a.m., a nurse came in, footsteps soft, as she set down a tray—semi-hard food, creams, and other disgusting mush I'd long stopped trying to identify.

At 10 a.m., my morning toilet. They turned me around, wiped down the parts of skin that showed, cleaned my shit and piss, sponged me. I liked one of the nurses better. Her long, white-blond hair, so pale it seemed to hum with an electric glow, was tied back but spilled soft and untamed around the edges. It wasn't just routine scrubbing and wiping for her—it felt motherly. I wanted to ask if she was the one who'd brushed my teeth before. But I didn't.

The next four hours... Nothing. Zilch. The worst time. Then lunch. Then nothing. Rest. I was 22 years old; I didn't need rest.

At 3 p.m., someone would be discharged. Someone else admitted. It had nothing to do with me. Just the revolving door of people sicker or luckier than me. I watched a handful of older people die.

At 4 p.m., another doctor's visit.

At 5 p.m., a snack.

At 6 p.m., dullness.

At 7 p.m., dinner. Another plate of mush.

At 9 p.m., lights out. Night-night. Like I was a child being tucked in, except no one was tucking me in. Just another long, empty gap before tomorrow.

"You could be my granddaughter," some gray-haired lady would say.

Thank you, but no. I wouldn't make a very good one.

As a kid, I was happiest in the afternoons when the house was mine alone. There was nobody to spoil my fun, to break the spell of my movie, my book. So blissful. Eating fruit yogurts, drinking cold juice straight from the fridge. Panorama was such a quiet neighborhood that any noise from outside felt like an intrusion. The only sounds that came from inside were the rustle of pages and the murmurs of the house itself. If I heard footsteps or voices beyond the gate, panic crept in—the fear that someone might ring the bell, end my haven. I always reassured myself it was unlikely. But that day, my worst fear came true. Someone actually dared to ring it. I knew it couldn't be my mom or dad. They both had keys. Who was it? Then there was knocking followed by another bell ring. I barely breathed. Then I heard my grandfather's voice.

"Ayla, it's Grandpa. Open the door."

I didn't answer.

"Ayla, are you in there? I know you are. Open the door."

"Grandfather! I'm here, but Mom locked me in, sorry. I don't have the key," I lied, and I didn't care. I just wanted to be left alone.

"Are you sure? I've been on the bus for the past hour. Open the door."

"Sorry, Grandpa. No key. I'm sorry. You go now."

With him long dead, I kept asking myself—why hadn't I opened the door for him? Why did I do so many things that I thought were horrible but did anyway? That's what my whole life felt like. Doing things that weren't like me. Acting in a way I deeply despised. It was as if there were two Aylas: one of them normal, and the other one spiteful, immoral, wicked.

Uncared for.

A young woman came in today. She wore a white coat, so she looked like staff. I hadn't seen her before. My parents stood beside her, holding hands. She wore a compassionate demeanor. She stood at the foot of the bed, holding her clipboard.

"Did someone die?"

"Ayla, I'm Ilenia Laskaris," she said. "I'm your assigned psychologist and am here to assess your mental health. I was told that you survived quite the accident."

What a luscious name.

"Tell me about yourself, Ayla," she said. "How are you feeling today?"

"What's the difference between a psychiatrist and a psychologist?" I asked her. "I always mix them up. You the one handing out pills?"

My mother rolled her eyes while my father looked away. I threw up my hands in a silent 'What?'

"That would be a psychiatrist."

"So, you're not Doctor Laskaris?"

"Not a doctor. Just a mere mortal." She continued. "You probably have a lot of time to think. What are you thinking about?"

"Absolutely nothing.", I said.

"So, you are in a sort of meditative state."

"No."

"What then? You've been through severe physical trauma."

"There's nothing to say, Ilenia." I was forever going to call her by her first name. "Just lying here and waiting."

My mother snapped then. "Show some respect, Ayla, would you?!" And her eyes flicked toward the frigid woman, offering an apologetic glance.

Laskaris shifted her weight, scribbling something on her clipboard. My mother made a small noise in her throat, like a cough caught halfway.

"I can leave," Laskaris offered.

"Please don't," my mother said abruptly, her voice thin and taut. "She needs to stop acting like nothing happened."

"Yasemin," my father barked at my mother.

But it was too late. Laskaris raised her eyebrows, glancing back at me. "What do you think about that, Ayla? Are you pretending nothing happened?"

My mother's hands tightened at her sides, and I could feel her glaring. My father took a step back, retreating into the corner, removing himself from the situation.

I turned to Laskaris. "I don't understand the question."

Laskaris opened her mouth as if she was going to say something, but then thought better of it. She nodded instead, a small, slow motion, like she had just put something together.

My mother stepped toward the bed, hands on her hips now, trying to steady herself. "Where is—" she started, but then stopped. She let out a long breath through her nose.

"Are we done here?" I asked Laskaris.

"I think so," she said. "For now." She observed me for another moment, her expression softening again. "Take care, Ayla."

My mother turned to me, her lips pressed tight. "You should get some rest," she said.

The room was quiet again. I stared at the ceiling, at the faint lines in the plaster, waiting for something—anything—to happen.

After a couple of days, the psychologist came again.

"Why are you here?" I asked her.

After a pause, she spoke, her voice calm and measured.

"I'm here to evaluate you," she said, folding her hands in her lap. "To complete a psychological assessment and to answer the questions the police and the court have asked."

"Why are the police asking questions? Is that the procedure for drunk driving?"

"It wasn't just that, was it?"

I curled an eyebrow at her.

"There were other people involved. Psychoactive substances involved," she said and then added, "The police have already confirmed that."

"So what is the question?"

"Who was with you?"

"You mean who gave me the drugs?"

"The police will ask you that. I want to ask you about the people closest to you, what you remember, and how you ended up in that situation."

I turned away and told her to go. I was too tired, too worn out to deal with it. Just not in the mood. *You're not going to get anything from me, not-a-doctor Laskaris.* She would report everything to my father. About the men, the drinking, the fucking, and the snorting. I was sure. Everyone reported to my father. That's the sort of person he was. And then my father would come. He'd pressure me. I'd cry. It all felt like a bad movie. Those kinds of films were popular now—a self-destructive hero or heroine you couldn't help but root for. You wanted them to hit rock bottom so they'd have a big realization and fix themselves right up. It was satisfying, seeing the happy ending after all the mess and mischief. It made the torture worth it. Even fun.

That was never my life. Never a positive twist. It was just a constant sinking—down into the abyss, to the very bottom. And when you reached it, you would think, *There's no other way but up*. Only to discover that the bottom was made of sand, and you kept slipping deeper. Darkness engulfed you, and you reached another bottom, even lower than the one before. And again, you would think, *There's no other way but up*. But there was always another abyss below. Each one darker, each bottom more horrible than the last. It was a never-ending decline.

Maybe that's what death was. Maybe it had already come for me. Every day I heard how lucky I was to be alive, but I felt like I was lying on my deathbed.

He came in then.

"Hi. Ayla, is it?" he said. "I'm Pappi. I will be your physiotherapist for the next couple of months."

I knew that voice.

"You know I've actually seen you before," he added, almost casually.

Oh, but I knew.

"I was there when they brought you to the emergency room. Glad to see you survived. You look… better now."

02: THE MOST DANGEROUS GAME

There wasn't any grand trauma to explain the path that led me here. At least not one I could recall. My father wasn't a handsy father. No leering stepfather crept into my room at night. None of that. But stories were hungry things. They'd eat the space you left for them. Laskaris asked about my childhood. She probably thought the answers were buried there, deep in the dirt, waiting to be unearthed. Psychologists and psychiatrists; they always thought so. And I gave her a version. I ornamented my memories, twisted them, set them aflame like offerings. For her entertainment? No—for mine.

There was Uncle Kostas, the nudist, my aunt's best friend. Every summer, I stayed with my mother's sister at her house in Chalkidiki. The days were long, the sea was warm, and Kostas was there, same as ever. He had brown skin from years in the sun and a balding head. He laughed a lot. Always had a joke ready. People liked that about him. He was harmless. Or so it seemed.

One day, all of us went to the beach, and we were swimming together, me and him, far from shore, where the water turned darker. "Don't worry," he said, his voice thick with his Thessaloniki accent. "I've got a tiny boat for you to hold on to if you get tired." And that was true; he actually said that. But I told Laskaris he threatened me: *touch me or drown.* I told her my small hand trembled as it moved where he directed. That he grabbed me, too. I watched her eyes widen when I said it. I watched the subtle twitch of her lips, the way she tried to hide her reaction. *You're good at this,* I thought, *but not that good.* It was a lie, of course. All of it.

It was my fifth lie to my psychologist. I was just getting started.

I knew everyone lied—but not like me. I lied the way people breathed. Without thought, without effort. The way we gulped air when it was there, as much as we needed, and sometimes even more than we needed. I lied to my parents, to my friends, to doctors, nurses, and teachers, to boys I liked, and to men I didn't like. There were just no consequences. Or, at least, there hadn't been. I lied to a boy once claiming I'd killed a puppy in cold blood, hammered its skull with a rock. "Probably that's why I behave strangely sometimes," I'd said. He believed me. He even fell in love with me. They always did when I lied.

Did she believe me, my psychologist? Maybe. Maybe not. I couldn't tell. She had a face like a mask—smooth, pleasant, impenetrable—except for her eyes. They betrayed something. I couldn't tell if it was pity or detachment. Or maybe she wasn't that good at her job, after all. She was young. Too young, working in a place like this. She said she had to write a psychological assessment for the police. That put me off, at first. But I talked anyway. To see how far I could push her. To see what she'd do with the pieces I gave her—how she'd shape them, whether she'd spot the lies or let them slide. I knew I was playing a dangerous game, but I was never one to shy away from temptation.

"Do they always assign people like you for cases like mine?" I asked her.

"What is your case?" she asked back, calm.

"You know. Alcohol. Drunk driving. Drugs."

"Not always."

"What makes my case special, then?"

She didn't answer. Not directly. She smiled an almost-smile, and said, "We'll get to that."

And then she asked me, "Can you name all your family members, Ayla?"

"Including crazy uncles?"

"Why not? Anyone you could name."

She handed me a pen and paper to keep track.

"Yasemin Sahin, my mother. Eren Sahin, my father."

Laskaris nudged me to continue. "Keep naming other relatives."

I began listing names—uncles, aunts, scattering them in circles around the page. Grandmothers and grandfathers, cousins I knew, and others I'd only heard about. A constellation of names, some familiar, others strange and distant. Some felt like names etched into a family tree I'd never climbed; others were ghosts I wouldn't have recognized if they sat across from me at a table.

"Do you often gather for family reunions? Big family dinners?" Laskaris asked.

"Sometimes," I said. "We used to, but not lately."

"How did such gatherings look? Feel?"

"Noisy," I said. "And tedious." I glanced down at the page, the pen still hovering over a name I hadn't finished writing. "Clattering plates, spilled wine, drunken men shouting over each other. Glasses filled and refilled. Old people spitting while talking."

"In Turkish tradition?"

I scoffed. "Hell no. Greek. We were never religious like that. My mother was born here."

Laskaris's pen stopped mid-scratch on her notepad. She looked up, waiting for something.

"What would you do on those occasions?"

"I dunno." I shrugged, the memory sliding in and out of focus. "Hide under the table. Be shushed. Run outside."

"Alone?"

"Mostly." I paused, the edge of the pen tapping against the page. "Unless the cousins were there too."

Her eyes lingered on me, waiting, but I didn't look up. I could already feel her next question hovering. And finally she fired her gun.

"Ayla, does the name Selen ring any bells?"

"Selen who?"

"Selen Sahin."

I knew she was closing in on something, and I was half-expecting that name to come up. "I ask you again. Who's that?" I pressed. "The cat's out of the bag, doctor. Who is this person you keep asking me about? What's with all the fucking secrecy?"

"Still not a doctor," Laskaris said calmly, her tone maddeningly even. "Who else has asked you, Ayla?"

"Her." I jabbed a finger toward the door just as my mother burst through it like a storm breaking glass.

"Ayla," my mother said, her voice cracking mid-word, high and desperate. "How can you not remember? Seli. You don't remember her? You don't know where she is?" Her breath hitched, rising to a wail.

"Tell me you know!" she demanded.

Was my mother eavesdropping the whole time? Or did that pretend-doctor tell her to hide behind the door? It was kind of funny, my mom hiding herself, trying to weasel her way into my session with Laskaris. *Bad girl you are, Mother.*

Laskaris fixed my mother with a stare so cold it could've frozen her mid-breath. If a look could kill...

But little did she know my mother did not care for some poor woman's opinion of her. Because my mom measured worth in thousands of euros.

"What is she talking about?" I asked Laskaris.

"Okay, that's enough for today."

"Not enough. I still don't understand," I said.

"Your sister. My daughter! Your sister, who hasn't been home since your accident." My mother's desperation seeped through her words.

Laskaris almost physically pushed her away. She told her something outside and came back to me.

"Don't beat yourself up, Ayla. We'll talk about it soon."

I was tired—bone tired—lost in a way that felt endless. Sleep tugged at me, heavy and insistent, settling over me like warm rain.

"Has my father been here today?" The question came out before I could stop it, surprising even me.

She answered that, to her knowledge, no. But she would ask the nurses. Then she left.

I couldn't blame him for not wanting to be here. A daughter like me was a father's worst nightmare. Maybe I had finally done it. Maybe the already rusted faucet of his love had run dry.

I glanced at the calendar, one of those cheap paper things stapled to the wall, curling at the corners. The date stared back at me, loud, smug. February the 14th. That goddamned day. That stupid, stupid day.

It didn't mean much when I was little—just paper hearts and chocolate. I was probably thirteen when it started to feel different. I remember not going to school that particular February. What was the point? The halls would be decorated with hearts and glitter. Stupid paper cupids, pink and red lurking everywhere. A massacre of love. There'd be those girls with their helium balloons and bouquets of cheap plastic roses, giggling like they'd won something. Boys passing notes or chocolates to the ones who had the right kind of hair or the right kind of smile. I didn't have any of that.

Instead, I skipped classes and went to the library, where I stuffed books under my jacket—books I wasn't planning to return. Once outside, I packed them all into my backpack. The baptism of my career as a klepto. Mostly Dostoevsky. Heavy stuff. Books that whispered, *You're not alone in the mess of it all.* A random woman followed me halfway onto the street, called me "a thieving little bitch," and threatened to report me if she saw me again. I got home, went straight to my room, and threw my backpack on the floor. The stolen books spilled onto the carpet. I was alone in the big house. Always alone during those years. I felt so bored.

In front of the standing mirror, I lay sprawled on my bed—legs loose, neck angled—studying my body's reflection. My clothes were in a heap on the floor. My gaze drifted past the mirror, to the bare window. With the lights on, I was on display. Anyone could see inside.

I sat up, the mattress shifting beneath me, and crawled toward the window. I pressed my face against the cold glass and peered out.

Who could be watching? Who could see me? A pervert. A father. A boy. A girl. A killer. A maniac. A frigid old man. Who were all those men I could not see? Noticing. Me. Having strong feelings about me. How I craved to have men go mad over me. They were all my Valentines.

I played my little show; took off my clothes by the window, folded them on the chair, pretended I was being watched. I turned my hips left and right naked in front of the mirror. In front of all the villains and uncles in the world.

And that night, after my parents were asleep, I slipped out. The streets at that hour felt alive in a way they never did during the day—empty but charged. That kind of quiet hummed with potential. I walked slowly, letting the cool air soak into my skin, looking for something I couldn't name.

It didn't take long before a car slowed beside me.

The window slid down with a mechanical whir. The driver leaned over. He was maybe forty, maybe younger—his face was red and bloated like he drank too much beer. "Need a ride?" he asked, his tone casual, almost bored.

I stopped. My heart kicked once, hard, but I didn't move. I saw that the car was packed with men. The driver pushed the door open just slightly, the hinges groaning. His hand hung out the window, palm up, calling me.

"Come on in," he said.

I stepped closer. Close enough to see inside.

It was one of those right-hand-drive cars – probably bought cheap and shipped from the UK; the kind you sometimes saw on the roads, but rarely in this neighborhood. The man in the passenger seat turned to look at me, then twisted awkwardly to climb into the back. The men in the back shifted to make space, their knees knocking into each other as they shuffled around.

"There's room for you now," the driver said, patting the seat next to him. "See? All yours," he said, glancing at me sideways, sizing me up.

The man in the back, nearest to the door, grinned, a cigarette tucked between his lips. "Hop in," he said. "We don't bite."

I hovered there, my body half-leaning toward the car, one foot planted firmly on the curb. "We'll take you to a party," the driver said. His voice was soft and coaxing, like he was offering me candy. "We'll take good care of you."

I could see the men's eyes—dark, glassy, and fixed on me. Not curious, not even impatient. Just… waiting. I could feel my heart pounding, quick and loud. I wanted to go with them.

"You coming or what?" the man in the back pushed, tapping ash from his cigarette into a beer can. For a moment, I thought I saw his tongue flick against his teeth. And I stood there long enough for the moment to shift, the men's faces hardening into something less inviting.

"I'm waiting for someone," I muttered finally, stepping back. "Thought you were them."

"I don't believe you. Come and spend the night with us," the driver said. But I moved further away from the car.

The car lingered a moment longer, and the door slammed shut. Then it sped off, its taillights bleeding red into the darkness, leaving me alone on the steep sidewalk.

A part of me wanted to call them back. The what-ifs swirled through my head, fast and thrilling. What if I'd gotten in? What if I'd let them take me wherever they wanted? I felt the imprint of their eyes on me, that awful, delicious pull of being noticed. Of being wanted. For a moment, I'd been standing on the edge of something dangerous, and I could still feel it humming through me.

This was the kind of story I would tell Laskaris—but of course, in my version, I entered the car. And there would be a spectacular gangbang.

Did all of that happen with my sister beside me? A ghost standing right next to me by the open door. Was she the one who stopped me, her hand grazing my arm? Or had she whispered, *Go on— let's get in*? For a moment, I couldn't trust the memory. Maybe I had entered. Maybe the car's mouth had swallowed me whole, and the rest of it lay buried somewhere in my mind, dark and waiting.

I stayed with the past a little longer, trying to bait her to the surface, to part the swamp waters of my memories and fish for my lost sister.

03: TELEPHONE TALES

At home, sex had been the taboo of taboos. The elephant in the room, sitting on the dinner table, growing fatter and more awkward with each passing day and year. I started reading when I was seven. That was how I got my sex education, twisted through the lenses of novels. My father took pride that I was such a ferocious reader. Books were my way out. Whatever the next fucked-up thing I did nobody could deny me my volume of read passages. Nor the number of men I've been with. My two big accomplishments. One of the men told me once, "Because you are smart and cute, you think you can get away with anything. You're just a little bitch and nothing else." True. Still, I was loved—too much. More than I deserved. Loved passionately. In every possible way. Adored. But not by the most important man.

Barely in sixth grade and boys had started calling the house. The landline at 7 Kampouridou waited, an open line of possibility, just waiting to ring. Sometimes their voices trembled with anticipation; sometimes they spat out insults, calling me a *little whore* while we were having dinner. I still remembered the digits of that old landline as if they'd been burned into me, 912671. How could I remember that, but not the sister who had perhaps been sitting at that same table? Who'd perhaps picked up that phone?

I behaved inappropriately; groped and kissed boys in bathrooms. Most of the boys hadn't complained; some had even looked for it, but it took only one whiner to have my mother brought in immediately. Our school had a reputation to keep. As you could imagine, that didn't make me very popular among the girls either. And rich girls in rich schools were as kind as terrorists.

"Know your price," my mother would tell me often when she didn't approve of me. Wasn't there something fundamentally wrong with that? *Know your price*. As if the more expensive you were, the more worth you had. Wasn't that trade reserved for exactly the kind of person my mother wordlessly accused me of being? My price, Mother? I gave myself for free, to whoever would take me.

My mother was made out of sand. I was made of liquid. Her roots came from the desert. Mine from the sea. We were just not meant for each other.

My mother knew the place of a woman in the family. Severely dominated by men, my mother was confused in the beast-world she had entered. Weren't Turkish women supposed to be good mothers? Wasn't that their fundamental quality? My mother was not being faithful to her culture. Maybe because she was an immigrant.

Maybe because none of us were faithful to anything—not really. Not to each other. Not to ourselves. *Be proud of your parents. Be proud of what we have*, my mother would say. And I must have sounded insufferable, running down the corridors and bragging about how much money we had. No wonder kids beat me up.

I learned from my mother how to lose—how to sit in failure like it was furniture, a place to rest. And I was there, sunk into that same velvet sofa, when the school principal called our home. This time, my father picked up.

He was summoned to school, where he was told a story about his daughter's outrageous behavior.

The story was about a physics professor who visited my high school—"a genius," they called him. He came to recruit a few of us for his summer camp. There was even a documentary about him and his camps on TV, making the whole thing feel more important than it was. He had Einstein hair and a wobble in his voice. He told us we were "special," that we were "portals," not just brains but gateways to the future, which sounded profound until you tried to figure out what it actually meant. "I'm not here to fill the bucket of your minds," he insisted, pacing in front of the whiteboard with his hands stuffed into his pockets, elbows jutting out. "I'm here to ignite the torch. To help you open the portals."

But then he got serious. His voice dropped.

"Be aware," he whispered, like he was sharing a secret. "Early sexuality closes the portals. Twelve- and thirteen-year-olds who experiment with… adult things? They rob themselves of their future. This is a crime. Against you, and against childhood itself."

His words aggravated me. Possessed me. Who did he think he was?

I raised my hand, and he gestured for me to speak.

All my life, I've envisioned myself leaping headfirst into wild, unthinkable situations. I thought, what if I were to take my clothes off now? Or when ambassadors and other consuls visited our house, what if I went into the middle of the room and screamed with all my strength? Or smashed the wine glasses lined neatly on the table, one by one, just to see their faces as the polished façade shattered? I imagined the chaos I could conjure, the ripple I could send through the carefully arranged world. I had never acted on those fantasies. Until now.

"It's 10 a.m., and my portal feels wide open." I had taken off my panties and eased my legs apart where my freshly shaven cunt gaped at him. *Spare me the judgment, Genius Man. You're just as deep in this filth as I am.*

I kept my face blank, but my voice was pointed, like I'd attached a string to those words and aimed them straight at his chest. His smile froze, then disappeared entirely. He looked at me like I'd just proven whatever theory he was working with. And maybe I had.

I took the long way home. Kicked at stones, smoked a cigarette, watched the sky go dark. It didn't matter. By the time

I walked through the door, my father had already gotten the call.

He was waiting in the kitchen, leaning against the counter, his arms crossed tightly across his chest like he was trying to contain himself. His tie was gone; his shirt sleeves rolled up, revealing his forearms, which he usually kept hidden beneath his suits. My father always looked put together, even when he was furious. His hair, thick and silver at the temples, was combed neatly back, his shirt still tucked in. The only sign that anything was wrong was his jaw. He looked like he was just about to spit. Probably at me.

He didn't say anything right away, just stared at me, his face turning redder the longer I stood there.

"What?" I finally said.

"What?" he repeated, his voice low and vibrating with some barely contained energy. "That's what you have to say to me? After what I heard today?"

I dropped my bag onto the floor. "What did you hear?"

"Oh, don't play innocent," he snapped, straightening up and stepping toward me. My father was tall, but he seemed even taller now.

"Do you have any idea what kind of disgrace you're bringing to this family?" he asked.

I flinched, not at the words but at his tone. It wasn't his diplomat voice, the calm, measured one he used when he was dealing with difficult people or trying to defuse an argument. This voice was raw, splintered.

"You're overreacting," I said.

"Overreacting?" Suddenly, he stepped up to me, and before I could do anything, his palm slammed hard into my cheek. "This is the third time I've been dragged into that school to talk about your behavior. The third time! Me!"

I folded my arms, matching his posture, trying to look bored, like none of this mattered to me. But my throat felt tight, and my arms started to loosen from their crossed position. Tears rolled down my cheeks.

"You swine," he said, his voice low and even, almost careful. "Everything I've worked for—everything I've built—for what? You're not what a daughter is supposed to be."

There was zero love in his words. Daddy and I. He'd bring me to a swimming pool when I was little, barely able to swim. And he hated staying in the sun like that, and he hated swimming pools altogether. But he'd do it for me, and for his own joy of watching me be happy.

It was almost comical how he insulted me now. A swine. The same man. My father never spoke like that. He was a diplomat. But it was okay. My manners were exquisite, my feelings unreadable. Expensive schools had trained me well. My wits had carried me through disrespectful men, through vigilant girls, through pain, separation—even through my own death in my father's heart.

I turned and walked away, not because I wanted to but because I didn't know what else to do. I made it to my room before the tears came again, slow and hot, as I leaned against the door. Downstairs, I could hear him moving around the kitchen, opening and closing cabinets, probably making himself a drink. By tomorrow, this would all be buried under the weight of whatever new crisis came along. That was how it always went with my father: moments of fury, quickly swept away and never spoken of again. But this time, something felt different. Something had shifted, like a wire snapping under too much tension. And I wasn't sure it could be fixed.

I broke up with my father then—or more precisely, he left me. I was ready to move on to men who wanted me. And I did so with hunger.

I demanded to talk to Laskaris.

"Why would I forget my sister?" I asked her. It was just the two of us, no parents hovering nearby. "Did my brain melt into mashed potatoes or what?"

"It's a neurologist's job to assess and diagnose any potential damage to brain tissue or neurological function."

"And your job then?"

"To determine the patient's current psychological status," she replied.

She hesitated, looking at me closely. "Sometimes the mind… has ways of hiding things from us. Imagine a jigsaw puzzle where the central piece is missing, preventing the full picture from emerging. Your mind has hidden the piece that represents your sister. A concrete blank spot on a concrete subject."

I looked down, picking at a loose thread on the blanket.

"That is how one suppresses a scene," she said, and then added, "or scenes—of violence. There still remains a certain tension though. A sense that something has happened, but we can't quite put our finger on it. We can't reach it. Like phantom pain."

I raised my eyebrows.

"A sensation of pain that feels like it's coming from a part of the body that is no longer there. It typically occurs after an amputation," she explained.

"Will I remember her?" I asked Laskaris. "Eventually?"

"I don't know, Ayla." Her voice dropped to a whisper.

"Do rape victims remember?"

"First, not always. Second, sometimes it is better if they don't."

I could feel something tightening in my chest. "Isn't there anything I can do? A pill I can take?"

Laskaris shook her head. "For now, we just wait. Let it come back when you're ready."

"Younger or older?" I asked her.

"Pardon?"

"Selen. Is she younger or older?"

"Selen was your older sister."

"Was?"

"I'm sorry–she is. Selen is your older sister."

"How much older?"

"Four years."

"Where is she now?"

"We will talk about that too."

"Why wait?" I asked, my frustration growing.

"You don't remember her. What difference does it make?"

I think she tested me to see if I was telling the truth.

"Is that why the police are circling?"

"Yes, that is why the court is involved as well."

Laskaris always had her notebook, and it was always closed. Balanced neatly on her lap, like she didn't need to write anything down because she already understood me, had me figured out. But I imagined her later, alone in her office, flipping it open, pen in hand, filling in the blanks with what I had or hadn't said. I wanted her to crack, to reach for that notebook while I was sitting right there—to prove I was outrageous, complicated enough, deserving of ink on the page. I began talking about past relationships, some borrowed from memory, some stitched together from lies.

But she just sat there, watching. Waiting.

"So, do you presently have a boyfriend? Anyone special?" she asked.

"No."

"Why not?"

"Just not how it goes for me." I shrugged.

"Never?"

"Well, not never."

"Do you remember your first?" she asked, leaning in now.

"Who doesn't?" I said. "I heard somewhere that we always remember our first. Always. But never the second."

"Your first man, or your first... experience?"

"Experience?" I mocked her. "Not sure. Man, I suppose."

"So do you remember your second?"

"Second man or second... fuck?"

"The second man you've been with."

I thought about it, then laughed, sharp and sudden. "I actually don't. For the life of me, I can't say who my second was."

"There you go," she said, with the slightest lift of her eyebrows. Then, after a beat, said, "Some psychoanalysts argue the first time is imprinting. That it sets the stage—for what we crave or what we don't like, what we repeat, what we can never seem to get enough of."

"I actually have two first times."

I was thinking of my first time in the cinema. I ditched classes and headed down to the multiplex. Something I did often; ditching classes and riding in taxis. Taxis as cheap as a sandwich.

By then, my hormones had turned me into something molten. I'd lie awake at night, waiting for my parents to fall asleep, then flick on the TV to watch porn. I'd fantasize about all my father's friends. I'd imagine being in a relationship with my teachers, my Lit teacher especially. So much teenage cunt saliva had dripped over thoughts of him. I developed scenarios. I told the girls about him. How it was forbidden but sweet. How his breath tasted of cigarettes and coffee. I told my cousin about the lint that clung to his belly button, the wiry hair curling around it. They stared, suspicious, unsure whether to believe me. But I kept, like a girl who knew what was what. And they asked me things, wanted to know how it felt, what to do, what not to do. I held answers.

My hair was pulled too tight that day. So tight, it hurt. I didn't remember the movie, just that Anne Hathaway was in it. What a stupid face. I always sat in the front row, even when the theater was empty. Especially when it was empty. Right up close, where the screen swallowed me whole. I held a giant Coke in one hand, the other tucked under my jacket. Pretending to watch, but actually getting myself off. My cheeks burned. My skin swelled.

A man sat next to me. I didn't see him come—suddenly he was just there, sliding into the seat beside me. His hand slipped under my jacket before I even had time to register what was happening.

It was rough and perfunctory. His grip found flesh with a sure, brutal efficiency, fingers digging hard and fast like he'd done this before. He moved deeper, his hand pushing between my legs as he crouched just enough to get better leverage. A raw burn radiated through my core. The pressure was unbearable. I couldn't move. I couldn't breathe. My pulse rang with an animal excitement indistinguishable from dread, panic, a flood of adrenaline, as if my life was at risk.

The screen flickered in front of me, its glow painting strange shadows across his face. A scene played—laughter, dialogue, music—so normal, so utterly disconnected from what was happening in the dark.

For an absurd second, I wondered if he was good-looking, if his face matched the casual cruelty of his hands. At least he wasn't old. And I wasn't thinking about him; I was thinking about what his hands were doing, what they were taking.

His fingers drove deeper and the pain sharpened, a horrible pressure building that blurred into a sensation I couldn't fully name. My stomach churned and heat prickled behind my eyes. I thought I might piss myself; the urge to empty my bladder surged as every muscle clenched to its limit. His fingers jabbed deeper, forceful, rougher with every second. Something close to pleasure.

I looked at him, but he didn't even glance at me. I reached out, tried to touch him, but he just pushed my hand away, cold, like I was nothing. Like I wasn't even there.

Then, just as abruptly as it began, it was over. He withdrew his hand, stood up, and walked off, leaving me crumpled in my seat. As if he'd never been there in the first place. Like nothing had fucking happened.

That was it—my virginity was taken not by a dick, but by a hand.

Later, in the bathroom, I pulled my panties down and found blood. Just a stain, dark, drying—spreading at the seams like a Rorschach test. A meaningless blot, or maybe not. I stared at it, trying to decipher something in its shape. But no pattern emerged, no message revealed itself.

I went to the cinema every day for two weeks with the hope he would be there. He never was.

I wanted the years of idling over. It was time for the real deal. The waiting would stop and real life would begin. Guys interested in me had their hearts broken. Guys that weren't broke mine. The intensity of my feelings, of my love and of my hatred, was as consuming as rabies.

My first time with a real dick was at a party. When asked, I tell people I was fifteen when I first did it. The truth is I was fourteen, and there is a slight chance I might have been thirteen. Drunk, sloppy, uneducated sex. And this unremarkable experience opened my appetites for the good version of that, whatever that was.

I was a woman now, but what followed didn't feel like womanhood. And that person didn't feel like me either.

I saw a boy who took me for walks. Long walks. I offered up. We went to bars at night, and we drank vodka and ate chips after that. I met a boy with condoms in his pockets. I met a man who knew me as a child. Who knew my father once. Who said, *"You're a fine-looking woman now."* Who said, *"Come with me, live in one of my apartments."*

No.

I met a man who was a priest. He wanted us to pray and then it would be okay to do it. I met a guy who said he'd pay me by the month. No is what I said.

I saw a boy who hit me. He bruised my eye in plum. I met a guy who said, *"Hey little red riding hood, what are you doing out so late at night?"* I met a guy and shortly after I had to wash my mouth with soap. A stupid thing. And I met a boy. And I met a man. And I lay down. And cried and whined and dined. I had so many men and many more.

"Don't worry, Ilenia. This is not going to be a sad story. This is just the intro."

Help me God for I have sinned.

04: SOMETHING WICKED THIS WAY COMES

"Ayla, was it?" he said. "I'm your assigned physiotherapist. You can call me Pappi."

The name was ridiculous.

Often, when I met someone new, my first thought was whether I would sleep with them. It was my instinctive reaction to people. There was this scanner in my mind that went over each part of the man's body. I'd done the same thing with the rest of the medical personnel. The doctor, an eight. But the young one whom I rarely saw—my doctor, with the purple circles around his eyes, a three. Antonis next door, a solid eight. Lit teacher, a ten. History teacher, a pathetic two. I would apply the ten-point scale to everyone. It was clear to me how stupid that was, but I did it anyway. Pappi was tall—basketball-player tall—but wiry, as if the wind could pick him up and carry him away. His limbs, long and loose, moved with a kind of distracted grace, each seemingly out of sync with the others. There was something soft in his face, an almost embarrassing prettiness, and it wasn't just his face—it was his presence. He looked like someone who held doors open, who smiled at children in grocery stores. I couldn't decide Pappi's score, which was rare.

Years from now I still wouldn't be able to answer that question. But, by then, the question would have become futile.

"Call me Pappi?" I could not stop myself. "Physiotherapist by day, porn actor by night? Is it short for something? Petrus?"

"Just Pappi, please."

I would never get used to that name. "You have a real name?" I asked him.

"You get through that door on your own, and I will tell you."

First, he pulled the blanket to the side and gently massaged my feet. I hadn't felt human touch in so long. I am not counting the nurses or doctors, because theirs was not exactly human. But to be massaged after taking off the plaster cast, it made me feel alive. To feel a pleasant touch again was a privilege, a sensation I had once lost and was now being granted again. He stretched my muscles like old rubber bands, each movement making my joints crackle and pop with a dry, fibrous sound as he worked. All of me was my legs. The connective tissue slowly released in thin, sticky threads; muscle fibers loosening like pulled taffy. I could feel adhesions tearing loose, tiny micro-traumas along the muscle belly, the faint warmth of lactic acid building up and then draining away as blood vessels dilated in response. There was pain, a deep, dull ache under it all, but it was smothered by that syrupy pull, the strange, drugged-up heaviness of muscle tissue being coaxed back to life, inch by inch.

"Full muscle atrophy."

"Haven't been to the gym lately," I said in response.

"Can you wiggle your toes?"

I tried to, the ones on the right foot.

"Has anybody asked you to do this during your check-ups?" he asked me.

"No. I don't even remember how long I have been here. I stopped looking at the calendar."

"Two months," Pappi said.

I looked at him while he looked at me. The massage went on, slow and methodical. Right leg, then the left, then my arms, my fingers. He pressed a couple of spots harder. I tried to read him—something, anything. Will I walk? Will I not? But he gave me nothing.

"What's the prognosis, doc?"

"I am not a doctor. We will see."

"One more not-a-doctor. Are we not in a hospital? Then what are you, a student?"

"You can say that, sure."

"Have you worked on a case like mine before?"

"You are my fifth patient for today."

"Fifth? Jeez! Am I the worst?"

"You might just be."

You could tell this was routine for him, just another body, another task. Had someone told him about me? About Selen? I wondered if the nurses whispered about it in the break room, leaning close, voices dropping to a conspiratorial murmur. Would he know the details, the real details, or just the outline of the story? And if the nurses talked, what would they say? Would they laugh behind my back? Would there be pity in their voices, or something else—something worse? I knew how people could be, how cruelty could wear a smile and hide behind humor.

If meeting Pappi was the first big thing that happened here—so unexpected, it left a kind of buzzing in my skull—the second big thing was seeing my sister.

I asked my parents for a photo of her. They gave me one, but my mother instructed, *"Hide this from Laskaris."* Her voice was low and secretive, and I savored the picture during those moments I was alone.

The photo showed a girl standing on a beach. She stood at the water's edge, her body angled toward the open sea, but her head was craned back at an odd angle to face the camera.

Her hair was blond—not just blond, but radiant, wrapping around her like a shawl. That blondness—it didn't sit right with me. With us. My mother had olive skin, her eyes nearly black; I had inherited her bold cheekbones and a dusting of freckles, but not her warm complexion. I was pale and raw by comparison, with unruly auburn hair that I'd hacked off in uneven chunks (a botched attempt at self-styling). Yet somehow, this girl, born of the same blood, had spun herself into gold. Was it my father's genes? Or had she just bleached her hair very successfully? A strange hollowness opened inside me, like the feeling of waking from a dream unsure of what is real.

I stared at the photo for hours that first day. And the next. Every day since. I couldn't stop. I kept it hidden—folded between the pages of an old book on the nightstand, slipped into my bag, tucked under my pillow. I would pull it out when no one was looking, always in secret, always careful. My initial instinct was to hate her. *What a cow*, I thought, which was always my reaction to women like her—too beautiful, too effortless, the kind of beauty that devours everything around it.

Then I imagined memories that weren't mine, as if I could slip her into my life and make her stay there. Sitting across from her at breakfast, sunlight pooling on the table. My hands on hers. My voice calling her name in some other place. In my mind, I was the one who took the photo that day on the beach, telling her to turn, to smile, to face me. Were we close? Sisters. Strangers. Both. I thought these things as if they were real, as if they had weight, planting memories of her cropped face in my mind while pushing out the ones that belonged there without her. I didn't care. The photo was mine now. She was mine.

At night, I'd lie awake, staring at the ceiling, imagining her life. She was out there somewhere—living, breathing, moving through the world. What did she do during the day? Did she find a job? Friends? A boyfriend? What did she eat for dinner? Did she laugh at stupid things? Did she ever look over her shoulder and think, for just a second, about me?

At first, I told myself it was enough to imagine her, to piece together her life in my head. But the more I thought about her, the more the photo felt like a lie. It was static, frozen. It didn't tell me anything I wanted to know. It didn't explain her or the pull I felt toward her, this knot of something tight and unrelenting in my chest. I needed more. More, more, more. I needed to find her. Not because I thought it would change anything—but because I couldn't go on like this, with nothing but a frozen image and questions that never stopped.

Pappi held my hand the first time I got up from the bed. Me and the bed, we were like a mother and a newborn baby. I'd forgotten how to be a separate being. The thing clung to me, or I clung to it, or we clung to each other in this weird symbiosis that probably meant something Freudian. Or maybe Jungian? Did Jung even have a take on beds? I'd have to ask Laskaris.

"Just one more step, okay? That's it. Two more for me," Pappi said, leaning close, his breath on my cheek. It made me think of grandmothers in parks, chasing after toddlers who wouldn't eat or wouldn't walk.

Pappi's case was peculiar. He wasn't really a physiotherapist. He'd gone to medical school, so I guessed you could call him a doctor if you wanted to dress it up. He didn't practice, though. Didn't seem to have the stomach for it, or maybe just didn't care enough. A year ago, one of his buddies crashed his Kawasaki. Bad. It was one of those bikes built to kill you fast and loud. Everyone had said the guy would never walk again, the nurses had told me. And Pappi fixed him. And after that, he remained at the hospital.

Turned out the guy was also tight with my doctor, the one with the sunken face and purple rings under his eyes. So now Pappi was here, floating around the hospital, doing his thing. The three of them—Pappi, the guy on the bike, and my zombie-eyed doctor—had some kind of bond, but no one ever told me what it was.

I walked. If you could call it that. Me, dragging myself forward, Pappi and the crutches keeping me upright. But still, I was upright, and the feeling was surreal. The nurses noticed me and hurried over, their faces tight with alarm.

"Miss! Go back to bed! Now!"

But Pappi didn't listen. With a quiet defiance in his posture, he whispered to me, "Don't mind them."

Later, he laid me back on the bed.

"Can I ask you something?" I said, a little hesitant.

"Shoot."

"Do you know about my... sister situation?"

He didn't look at me but nodded; a quick, clean nod like it didn't matter, as if I'd just asked him if he wanted coffee.

"Why didn't you say anything?"

"Laskaris told me not to. Told us all not to."

"You know she is missing and I have no memories of her?"

"That's about all I know, yes."

Silence settled between us, shifting the conversation.

"How long until I can walk on my own again? To be as before?" I asked him.

He hesitated, and I hated the hesitation more than the words that followed.

"At least six months," he said, and his voice was cold, precise. "Maybe more. You're not working hard enough. You quit too easily. At this pace, six months—if you're lucky."

Heat crawled up my neck. "What?"

He didn't answer.

"How do I cut that time in half?" I asked, louder this time. "I'd rather die than stay here for six more months."

"Don't be dramatic." His tone stayed infuriatingly calm. "You can leave the hospital long before that. But be diligent. Get up even when you're tired and push through the pain. Stop slacking off and move every chance you get. Right now, your muscles are softer than a kitten."

Soft, I thought. Yes, that was right. Soft like surrender.

"Also, I want to make one thing clear," he added. "I am not sure it will ever be *as before*."

I remained quiet for a second.

"You know, back in school, I played basketball. I was good—really good—but too inconsistent to stick with it. Mother and father never pushed me. So, around the tenth grade, I stopped. I still had regrets about it." A weak laugh escaped me. "For years, I had a recurring dream that I hadn't quit. Especially lately. In the dream, I'm in the WNBA finals, like I'm Lisa Leslie, and I hit a three-pointer at the buzzer. The crowd goes nuts, and my team lifts me on their shoulders, chanting my name. I always woke up wondering if I could've been that good—if I'd blown my only chance."

"Why did you stop?" Pappi asked me.

I shrugged. "Honestly? Laziness."

I wouldn't make the same mistake twice. I needed to walk, get out, and find Selen.

He shook his head. "I read a book once that said laziness isn't real—just fear in disguise."

I looked away, picking at the hem of my shirt. "I don't know. I didn't want to be disturbed. I liked my rest. My movies. My books. I preferred to stay home."

I paused, the memory tugging at me, deciding to get naked like that.

"On my very last practice," I said, "my dad drove me there, dropped me off right in front of the basketball hall... and I just didn't go in. Called a taxi, went straight back home. Did what I loved most." I swallowed, glancing down at my hands. "That was the last time I ever got to the court."

"You loved most?"

"Being inside my house, by myself. Watching stuff, reading."

"That sounds... empty," he said, studying me.

"One man's hell. Another man's paradise."

"Isn't the saying 'one man's trash is another man's treasure'?" he asked.

"Semantics. Here, I invented a new saying."

"Fair enough." Pappi smiled. "Me, I was always outside, running, messing around. Didn't matter what we played. Didn't matter with whom. Just being out there, in the burning daylight."

"Bet you had a big group of friends too. You look like that kind of guy."

He hesitated. "Not as many as you'd imagine."

We sat in silence for a moment, and then, before I could talk myself out of it, I asked, "How old are you, anyway?"

"Thirty-three," he said.

"Perfect age to check out."

He just stared. No laugh. No reaction.

"You know—Jim Morrison, Kurt Cobain, Janis Joplin. They all offed themselves at thirty-three." I added.

"You mean the 27 Club."

"What?"

"They died at 27. Not 33. Hence the name."

I rubbed my forehead. "So who died at 33? Why is that number stuck in my head?"

"Jesus."

"Oh, God." I groaned.

"Yeah. Exactly."

I let out a laugh.

"Anyway," I said as I gave up, "I never had that big of a crew like you guys did. I envied the hell out of that. I swear it's different for girls. I don't know why, but it is. Even when I was with the team, I had no one to talk about stupid shit. Maybe men are just better at not being assholes to each other."

"This doesn't sound like an objective remark."

"Yes, but the alternative is worse."

"What's the alternative?"

"That the problem lies with me."

He chuckled, smooth and knowing, like he'd heard this all before.

"I think I'd like to go back to university as soon as possible," I said, quietly, carefully, like the words might dissolve if I said them too loud.

"No wonder. I would too," he said. "Much better than being stuck in a hospital."

He didn't get it. He didn't know what college was for me—what it did to me.

05: MY MOTHER: DEMONOLOGY

"This will be the first and last time when professionals are paid, and not by you, to read and grade and tutor you. Each silly thing you produce, we are obliged to read. Now is that time. Take advantage." That was part of the speech at reception when they greeted us as freshmen.

"That's not entirely true, is it?" I turned to one of my roommates. "They are technically paid by us."

"More by our parents," she said with a laugh.

"Speak for yourself," I said, selling the lie like I'd busted my ass in three dead-end jobs and scraped together every last cent.

I shared a dorm with two girls, Ashley and Monica. American girls with light voices and light hair, both looking like they had stepped out of some glossy magazine. I wasn't driven by some great burning intellect or ambition. I was driven by want. The want to be free of my parents, away from the things they asked of me—be this, do that, stay here.

Pylaia wasn't far enough, not really. My parents still thought they had me leashed. They enrolled me at the ACT, perhaps to get me far away from the madness of Aristoteleio, where the police weren't allowed to enter the campus, and the parties were notorious and wild. My university was far enough to avoid the protests, the strikes, and the smashed beer bottles littering Aristoteleio's campus, where—as I'd been told—my sister used to study. That place was a student's wet dream. Everybody wanted in. Was she responsible enough that they trusted her with that choice, or was she a wreck like me? Did I go there often to see her? My first year should have been her last there.

My parents thought they could dodge a bullet by keeping me behind the red-brick building, white-trimmed windows, and a postcard-perfect view of the American College. It sat on a tranquil hill outside the city. Oh boy, how wrong were they. Little did they know how I was slipping the rope; what it meant to rake under their noses, to carve out that little rebellion. I burst that bubble, smashing through it with both fists swinging; the bubble they wanted to wrap their naughty little daughter in.

Madness travels light.

And it came with me in the Louis Vuitton suitcase I had packed too quickly, its gold zipper snagging on a folded dress, in the cigarettes crushed into the lining of my jacket pocket, and in the vodka I stuffed somewhere between all my bad decisions. By the time I arrived at the college, I could feel that madness again, threading through my body, turning my blood sticky, coating my fingernails in red.

We hit it off at the beginning with Ashley and Monica. The two girls would play such a part in my life, though none of us knew it then. But did anyone know, when we met, the shape we'd take in each other's lives? The reach of our own lives, stretching out past us, touching others like long silk scarves that catch on everything. All the light and dark we left behind. All the pain and pleasure merging until they were indistinguishable.

"I'd love to make you girls a Caesar salad," I would tell them. "I have a bomb salad dressing I got from the States. I brought with me like twenty bottles. It makes all the difference. You just get the iceberg."

Drunk on girl love, high on it like a new drug. I wanted to keep it, bottle it, never let it fade. It made me feel like the happiest girl alive. With them, I pretended I was American. And for a while, I almost believed it. Even acquired some of the accent, the lazy vowels, the slow-pulled words.

Many years later, I would contemplate how I was and how they treated me, rolling the tape over and over, different each time. And who was the villain and who the hero. I would draw in my mind all kinds of scenarios and conversations gone differently. It changed each time. In one version, I was the fool; in another, I was the casualty. In some, I fought back. In others, I let it happen. They set something in motion. A chain of bad choices, a spree of lies, a slow unraveling that carried me forward, through years I had not yet lived.

One night, I took Ashley's mascara, and she called me a *fucking klepto*. Monica was right beside her. Neither of them laughed. The word was like a curse cast between us. It separated us. Then it possessed me. As if I had decided to own it, to step into the role they had written for me.

From then on, I took things. Little things at first: makeup, jewelry, books. The want started as a whisper—*this is yours for the taking*—and then it grew.

I let my fingers drift over counters, inside purses, across shelves. Not searching, just waiting. Then finally, I became bolder.

I saw the bag sitting on the table next to mine, half-hidden under a damp napkin. It caught my eye—one of those shimmery little clutches, stitched together from sequins, catching the light like a lure. The bar was packed, everyone jammed shoulder to shoulder under the neon lights and the weird orange glow they used for "atmosphere," which mostly just made it look dingy. A bunch of us from campus were there, spilling into booths and crowding the bar counter; everyone pretending to be a little drunker than they actually were.

The clutch was small with a flash of metallic teal. The two girls who'd been sitting at the table had already wandered off halfway to the dance floor, giggling over something. Their drinks were still sweating onto the wood, slowly pooling into sticky rings.

No one was watching me. Everyone was focused on the pulsing music, the blaring bass, the tangled mess of voices rising and falling. I could feel this low hum start in the back of my head, like something awakening; the kind of thrill I used to get sneaking out of my house late at night while my parents slept, knowing I'd get away with it. I didn't even think. My hand just drifted out, fingers brushing the bag's cool, slick surface.

I then slipped the clutch off the edge of the table and let it dangle against my hip like it belonged to me. It was heavier than it looked. I didn't open it right away. Just kept it close, the weight settling against me like a secret, a quiet sort of possession that no one else knew about. I felt the burn of anticipation in my stomach; the heat curling up into my chest as I headed toward the back of the bar where the crowd thinned out near the bathrooms.

Then, in the shadows, I popped the clasp open, feeling the faint resistance before it gave way with a soft click. Inside, a faint whiff of floral perfume, a tube of lipstick, a crumpled receipt, a phone with a cracked screen, and a tiny, red wallet that looked like it had seen better days. My fingers traced the worn leather slowly, savoring the moment. I didn't know why I wanted it—I just did.

I slid the wallet out and tucked it into my own bra, snapped the clutch shut, and left it right where I'd found it, empty now, barely there. I never took anything from stores—their cold, inert goods didn't tempt me. Only from people.

It wasn't a pathology. I was sure of it. Not really. But people made it into something real—a badge I could wear. And so I wore the sticker and took everything I could find—jackets in clubs, earrings, boyfriends.

Then someone called me crazy, and I played that part. Once, in some guy's room, I broke a bottle and pressed my hand straight into the glass.

I'm looking at the scar now, as I write this. To this day, I don't know why I did half the things I did. Why a single word from someone's mouth could become my whole identity. Why I took their insults and turned them into life choices. And I'd been called many things: a klepto, a wicked girl, a stupid thing, a little bitch, a whore, a devil girl.

What possessed me?

The truest answer I have is this—want. Want, stripped of reason. Want, raw and blind, tearing through me, burning through anyone who got too close.

But I couldn't think about other people's feelings—I was too wrapped up in my own pain. My hurt was the sharpest thing, the only thing that felt real; a constant ache, a drag of misery and anxiety. Craving for a breath of fresh air. Of laughing, of having a connection, of nailing an exam, of acknowledgement.

Dana and I spent two hours preparing in my room. It was a Friday, and I was looking forward to it. The electronic party was the weekend everybody was on campus. Dana was a Romanian girl I met online, and she was my party partner. She would come to Thessaloniki, and I would visit her in Bucharest sometimes. I liked to go there. No one knew me there. It was difficult to find anybody that would like to go out as much as she did. We clicked. She would come visit me. Dana was my debauchery friend.

We took a pill each and smiled at each other.

"I really like your hair," she said, running her fingers through it lightly, as if afraid it might break. Or maybe she was afraid that she would. We hugged, then kissed softly on the lips.

"I want a drink," I said. "I wonder if it's gonna make me feel bad."

"Maybe wait or get a really small one with juice if you're craving."

"I am craving," I said and winked at her.

It was so loud at the club that my words were left hanging on the waves of the music. The music started to sound better and better, with a crystal clarity that made me feel pure and happy. Just happy. I looked at Dana, and she was already in her own movie of sounds and light.

"You are so pretty. Like a lightbringer," she said.

"Don't they call the Devil that?"

"I guess the Devil is pretty too."

I've tried so many things. I smoked weed, I'd taken cocaine, amphetamines, MDMA. But ecstasy was the best. Synthetic happiness at its finest. Pure bliss raving on music and dancing and becoming one with the rhythm.

There were two guys circling us from the beginning. We didn't mind; it happened to us often. Dana started talking with one of them, but I didn't feel like it. I just wanted to dance and feel the music undisturbed.

After the pill wore off, we started drinking. The other one turned to me.

"Are you from around here?" he asked.

"No, just here for uni."

"You know, we've rented a really big house and there will be a DJ for the afterparty. Would you like to join us?"

I think he saw the hesitation in my eyes.

"Don't worry, we are good guys. Not one of these assholes that will hurt you." That should have set off the alarm, but it didn't. I felt reassured.

I couldn't say why I was looking for those words, and I certainly didn't know why the words calmed me down. I felt in good hands. An illusion of safety that was given so cheaply. After that day, I would run from those words, as if a mad beast was charging after me.

Dana and I went to the afterparty after briefly discussing it. It wasn't our first; we were experienced.

After partying all night, the guys gave us a room and said we could stay. I was on one bed, Dana on the other at the far end of the room. We talked a bit. I was thinking of asking her to come to me, so that we could sleep together, but I was ashamed. I should have snuggled next to her. Maybe the next thing wouldn't have happened.

Warmth woke me up. I still felt drunk, so I knew that little time had passed. My head was pounding. A hand touched my ass and something wet followed it. I was in a state between sleep and being awake.

"Mmm," he moaned. "So sweet. Ripe and ready."

Nausea rose in waves, thick and metallic, as if my body had become its own foreign terrain—something I inhabited but did not control. I was barely conscious, tethered to wakefulness by the faint, queasy awareness of sensation. A slick warmth traced along the curve of my lower back. My stomach pressed into the mattress, the sheets tangled and damp beneath me. At first, it seemed like a dream. The realization unfurled slowly, horrifyingly, like ink spreading through water. Fingers, hands—no, a tongue. My cheeks spread apart; he licked my ass and then inserted his tongue inside my vagina.

That was the *we-are-good-guys* guy.

Had I bathed? Was I clean? Why did my mind go there—of all things, why that?

"You're so hot," he murmured. "So wet. Dripping." Like he was trying to convince me I was turned on.

The words hit like something blunt and heavy—words meant to seduce but that made my stomach churn. The nausea curled in my gut, squeezing tight, but I couldn't move, couldn't twist away. My body refused me, a rebellion of its own making. Paralyzed, like those drugs I'd seen on TV—the ones that leave you fully awake, fully feeling, fully trapped.

I hated it, hated him, hated myself for the small, involuntary sound that slipped past my lips; a moan, not of pleasure but of something else entirely. Protest, despair, humiliation. But he took it as encouragement.

My body was a thing; a limp, heavy object that he turned over as if it were his right. Onto my back now. His weight pressed down, and his mouth came over mine—hot, forceful, wet. His tongue shoved past my lips, a kind of suffocation, and his beard scratched raw against the edges of my mouth, catching on my skin like sandpaper.

His hands moved to my breasts, kneading them in a way that was neither gentle nor rough; only deliberate, mechanical. He kissed one, then the other. Wet smacks that left my skin cold. His fingers slid lower, inside me, probing and relentless. "Such a sweet and wet and tight pussy," he said, his voice a rasp now, almost triumphant. "So delicious."

I wished to disappear.

He didn't seem to notice—no, he noticed, but he didn't care. He talked the whole time. "I like this," he said, his words mixing with those guttural breaths, those obscene little grunts. "God, you feel so good." His voice was too loud, the words hollow, ricocheting off the walls of my skull. Fear held my limbs immobile—not fear of harm, exactly, but fear of causing offense, of making a scene.

Abruptly, he took my hand and placed it on his erection. He waited for me to move, to respond. When I didn't, he gripped my fingers until they squeezed him. His skin was hot and sticky. "Just like that," he murmured. "You like that, don't you? You like my big dick?" His hand guided mine, moving it up and down along his penis; making it seem as if I was doing this, as if it was me.

When my hand stayed limp, when I still didn't respond, he shifted again, grunting as he positioned himself. The weight of his body came down on me, his chest pressing into mine. My body accepted him in the way it might accept a blow or a wound—passive, inert, as if there was no other choice. My mind hovered somewhere above it all, detached, watching from a distance as he started fucking me.

It could have been five minutes. Or five hours. The longest of times. The shortest of times. A blink.

And then I pushed him.

I said something, but by now, the words had dissolved, lost to memory.

"What do you mean..." he replied, trying to kiss me.

He didn't seem to want to listen to me.

I wish I had some alien super-strength to push this unknown man away.

"What's wrong with you, honey?"

"Please. Stop." I hated that I had to say the word. I was imagining I was cracking his skull, but instead I was saying *Please*.

"All is good. You're so sweet and pretty. You're so gorgeous. Let's have fun."

He finally let me go in anger. I know what he told himself, what he was going to tell his friends. *"The chick went crazy. We were doing it, she wanted it, not that she was good at it, and then snapped!"* That's the story he would choose. His memory of that night will never match mine.

I turned toward Dana's bed, and I saw her eyes open, which she quickly closed. *But I think of that moment. I think of it again and again.* She would say that she was asleep the whole time. *But I won't forget how our eyes met, Dana.*

I acted in the only possible way I saw before me, in ignorance. He would contact me on Facebook the next day. And the strangest part was that I was going to accept. Pretending nothing had happened. I didn't dwell on it at the time. Fuck it. I was an indestructible party girl. I even wrote a post on my Facebook. *Nick Fanciulli rocks.* That was the name of the somewhat famous DJ who played at the club. The fucking guy had the nerve to comment below it, *You rock.*

There was another version of that night:

I woke to the feel of his tongue—warm, wet, sliding down my back, slipping between my cheeks, pushing where it didn't belong. Panic took hold.

I kicked backward, hard, my heel smashing into something solid—ribs, face; I didn't care. He grunted, the weight of him peeling off me.

"What are you doing?" My voice ripped out of me, a snarl, a scream. "I'm fucking sleeping. Get off me! I'll kill you. I'll blow up this fucking house. Dana! Dana!" I shouted her name as if she'd save me. Although I already knew she wouldn't.

"You little cunt." His voice came from the floor, wet and ugly. He wiped at his mouth and spat blood. "Get the hell outta here. Before I—" I didn't let him finish. I stumbled to my feet, grabbed the first thing I could—a broken bottle, jagged at the edges—and swung it. His face opened up, flesh sagging like a peeled fruit, blood spilling so fast it pooled under him. And the gory, sweet smell of it was overpowering. He begged, then. Cried like a child. But I didn't stop.

There were two things I couldn't shake. First, the feeling that he was everywhere—on the streets of Thessaloniki, in the shops, at the cafés. I thought I saw him near the college too; his shape flickering in the crowd, familiar and wrong. Second, the image of his oily, stupid chin burned into my mind like an afterimage.

Whatever. Life didn't stop for paranoia. The days stacked one on top of the other until the semester was suddenly over.

Winter break rolled in, bringing with it a crisp stillness. It was my first day at home, and in the kitchen, my mother stood at the sink, washing lettuce.

"You know, they're full of nitrates, especially now," I told her.

"That is why I am washing them really well."

It was so boring to be home. Each hour carved out of marble. The world outside moved while I stood trapped in syrup. Home wasn't far from Pylaia—just twenty minutes away by car—but I almost never visited during those years. My parents' house was huge, silent, filled with expensive furniture nobody sat on and rugs so soft your feet would sink into them. The air smelled faintly of lilies, the artificial kind that came from a diffuser perched on a glass console table next to an art book no one ever opened.

My family home wasn't where fun went to die. It was where it had never lived. My mother lived in curated silence wrapped up in the idea of me she had crafted years ago—a respectable young daughter in a perfect frame. She still clung to that portrait, refusing to take it down, refusing to look too closely at what had replaced it.

"Would you like us to make baklava together?" my mother asked one afternoon. She was standing in the doorway of the kitchen, her voice too quiet, too gentle.

I stared at her for a moment, long enough for her fingers to tighten on the doorframe. "Not today," I said.

Her mouth opened, like she was going to ask something else, but then she just nodded and walked away, disappearing back into the kitchen. The air felt heavier after she left, the silence buzzing in my ears. I turned and walked upstairs to my room, shut the door, and lit a cigarette on the balcony. The first drag was bitter, the smoke curling around my face as I exhaled toward the sky. I stubbed out the cigarette halfway, disgusted by the taste it left in my mouth. My mind wandered to the most beloved memory I had of my mother. It was from a morning after one of my crazy nights. The hangover was bad, the kind that gripped your skull and squeezed, leaving the edges of the world blurred and sharp at the same time. I told her I was sick. I might've managed a fever—I didn't check, but I knew how to look pitiful when I needed to.

She didn't ask any questions, didn't scold or lecture me. Instead, she disappeared into the kitchen. I lay on the couch in the den, wrapped in a blanket that smelled faintly of detergent, listening to her move around—the clink of the spoon against the pot, the rhythmic sound of her knife on the cutting board.

When she brought out the bowl, the smell of it hit me first: broth, garlic, a hint of lemon. Chicken soup. She set it down in front of me on a silver tray, along with a glass of water and a cloth napkin folded neatly beside the spoon. "Eat slowly," she said, her voice soft, as if she were afraid the noise might make my headache worse. She sat down across from me with her tea, steam curling around her face.

She didn't say anything, just sipped her tea, her eyes flicking over me as if she were looking for cracks. For a moment, I felt like her child again, like I could close my eyes and this would all disappear—her questions, my excuses, the parties, the drinking, the way my life had spun so far off the track she thought I was on.

After I finished my soup, she soaked a towel in warm water, wiped my mouth, and ran it over my hands. Then she folded one of her expensive cotton napkins, dampened it with colder water, and put it over my forehead.

Charles Dickens wrote the following scene in *David Copperfield*, when David returned from a year at school:

> ...I went in with a quiet, timid step. God knows how infantile the memory may have been, that was awakened within me by the sound of my mother's voice in

the old parlour, when I set foot in the hall. I think I must have lain in her arms, and heard her singing so to me when I was but a baby. The strain was new to me, and yet it was so old that it filled my heart brimful; like a friend come back from a long absence. I believed, from the solitary and thoughtful way in which my mother murmured her song, that she was alone. And I went softly into the room. She was sitting by the fire, suckling an infant, whose tiny hand she held against her neck. Her eyes were looking down upon its face, and she sat singing to it. I was so far right that she had no other companion. I spoke to her, and she started, and cried out. But seeing me she called me her dear Davy, her own boy! and coming half across the room to meet me, kneeled down upon the ground and kissed me, and laid my head down on her bosom near the little creature that was nestling there, and put its hand up to my lips. I wish I had died. I wish I had died then, with that feeling in my heart! I should have been more fit for heaven than I have ever been since.

"*I wish I had died then, with that feeling in my heart,*" Dickens wrote, and I understood. A single moment of love so acute, so unbearable, it felt like a wound—a place you could disappear into forever.

My father, on the other hand, knew I was faking the whole sickness thing. I could see it in the tight line of his mouth, in the way he refused to meet my eyes when he passed me by on the couch. He didn't talk to me the entire day. But my mother—she stayed by my side, refilling my glass, pressing a cool cloth to my forehead every time I groaned a little too theatrically.

Winter fucking break. Twenty-four days of drinking, drinking, smoking, drinking again. Parties, weed, boys, drinking. Lines of coke on polished countertops. Circles of strangers around me, laughing and shouting under spinning lights. Glasses sweating in my hands. Hangovers that crawled over my body, leaving a sour taste in my mouth that wouldn't go away. All sins cruelly tearing at flesh and soul. And every time I came home, the house was quiet, too quiet, waiting for me to either collapse or confess the things I didn't know how to say. The kitchen light would be off, but I could see her there anyway, her shadow hovering, asking softly if I wanted to make baklava, as if sweetness could fix what was broken.

I clawed my way through the first years of college over the corpses of people who expected something of me. Fiends who stopped answering my calls, lovers who always wanted more, professors who looked through me with exhausted indifference. I was nobody's favorite student. None of that *stray-but-talented-student* archetype that we cheer for in the movies.

The first two years were all probation, like a seesaw: up one semester, down the next, until I learned to balance, just barely. A 2.1 GPA looked just right to me. They said I was on thin ice. I imagined it cracking beneath me, slow and clean, but it never broke. High school was no different. Ninth grade, tenth grade—a slow, steady dive into failure until I worked out the formula. The math of survival. How many assignments I could hand in at the last minute to stay afloat. How many mornings I could show up hungover without tipping the balance. Just enough sobriety to pass, to slip through unnoticed.

The parties all bled together. Same booze, same bullshit, same faces I couldn't tell apart. Boys whose hands I let wander in the dark—boys whose names I forgot before the sun came up. And the girls. Girls who'd been my friends once, until I decided they might be something else. I wanted them for reasons I couldn't explain, not to myself and definitely not to them. They looked better in the haze of vodka, easier to love—or maybe just safer to touch.

06: CRASH

Meanwhile, while I was raking, my first boyfriend had gone and died.

Truths: He really was my first—the first dick inside me, and the first awkward thrusts we pretended were passion. He said I was his first lover, too. I wasn't sure I believed him. We lied to each other all the time; it was part of the game. He told me he loved me once, over the phone, while I sat on the kitchen counter eating yogurt straight from the tub.

But Alexis didn't love me. Not really. He didn't treat me well. He ignored me for days, played games to keep me chasing. He flipped out when he saw me with his friends, got aggressive, yelled like I was something he needed to control. Not that I was innocent. I didn't treat him any better. I was a wreck—new to sex, new to booze, new to wanting things that didn't make sense to me yet. Coaxing possessive jealousy out of him on purpose. And the cherry on top? I had a little crush on his father, for God's sake.

We were on and off for a couple of years, but I hadn't seen him in a while. Until one of his friends called me and I went to the funeral. He had died in a violent car crash. But then again, is there any other kind? I had never been this close to death before, never looked directly into its face—until now. It resembled him in the coffin. Almost. But Alexis wasn't there. What lay in that box was something else, something bloated and stiff, a grotesque imitation of the boy I once knew and pledged my love to.

There were two other guys in the car that night. The driver, who survived unscathed. And another boy, Rafail, who we called Raf. He didn't get off so easy. The crash messed him up bad, but he lived. I was with him afterward, but it was a secret. Raf, who smiled like he was still surprised to be alive. Something about that accident made me want him, made me fall for him. As if being near him could pull me closer to the edge of something I couldn't reach on my own.

Stories I told people about Alexis's death:

Alexis and I had just decided to get back together. After years apart, we'd finally found our way to each other again. Now I was in mourning, wearing only black.

We ran into each other at a club. I went home with him, and we spent a week together; tangled in bed, talking like we hadn't missed a day. That happened right before the accident.

I drove the car. I killed him.

I was his wife. We had married in secret.

At the funeral, his father told me, "Dear, you were his first love." Oh, and I liked that so much. I let it wrap around me, warm and soft, something I could sink into.

Later, I would wonder if his accident had anything to do with mine. A divine revenge for dressing myself in his story. A subconscious desire to live what he went through. Didn't Laskaris say that you always remembered your first man; that the first imprinted on you for the rest of your life? The biggest magic trick of all. It was really scary to lie because all of the stories I told came true. Which was, of course, yet another lie.

I shared that story with Pappi, skipping the lying part. It was distant enough to feel safe, yet intimate enough to bring us closer.

"You should try keeping a journal," Pappi said, breaking the awkward silence that might occur after someone shares about their ex-boyfriend's death. His tone was casual, like it wasn't the first time he'd suggested it. "It might help you keep track of things. Fill in some of the gaps."

I didn't answer right away. The gaps he meant were obvious—my sister.

"Here, look," he continued. He paused for a moment, and then he pulled out his planner, flipped it open, and shoved it toward me.

"What am I looking at?" I asked.

He showed me his calendar. Every single day filled with notes crammed in without exception. The boxes that contained each day were oddly large as if the notebook had been custom-made. He handed it to me, and a faint whiff of detergent and antiseptic drifted off him.

There was something extraordinary in peering into a man's calendar. Something so alien and so intimate. It was the ritual of us becoming something more than a patient and a medical professional. A response to my plea. I took it quietly with great care and held it as I would a small bird, afraid to murmur a word.

March 12

6:30 a.m. First light through the curtains. Breathing exercises. Twenty seconds in, forty seconds out. I cheat. Coffee next. Black. Bitter. No phone, no screens, no noise. Fifteen minutes, watching the steam curl up and disappear.

7:30 a.m. Flaw review. Too stiff. Too blunt. Smile looks wrong, but no time to fix it. Just don't scowl. That's enough.

8:30 a.m. At the clinic. Mrs. Kallistratou, 74. Back pain radiating down her legs. I tell her to stretch. She sighs like I just asked her to climb Mount Olympus. Then Mr. Damianou, diabetic neuropathy. He listens, nods, smiles like he's humoring me. His shoes are too old. I want to say something, but I don't.

1:30 p.m. Lunch at my desk. Spanakopita from last night. It's cold in the middle, but I eat it anyway. Cursor blinks on the screen while I input patient notes. Did I update Mrs. Kallistratou's prescription? I can't remember. Maybe I did. Maybe I didn't. Either way, the thought sticks.

3:00 p.m. Home visits. Mrs. Pavlina, 91, stirring stew when I arrive. Arthritis in her hands so bad she shouldn't even hold a spoon, but she doesn't stop. "You need to eat," she says, pushing a bowl into my hands. I eat it. It burns my tongue. She tells me about summers on the coast, the oregano fields, the goats. Her voice shakes, but her hands don't.

Then Mr. Filippou. Ex-construction worker. Says he used to climb scaffolding like it was nothing. Now he wheezes crossing his living room. The remote doesn't work, so I fix it. He pats me on the shoulder like I just saved his life. His house smells like onions.

6:30 p.m. Back home. Dinner. Something microwaved. Chew slowly, stare at the wall. Blood pressure cuff sits on the table. I don't touch it.

8:00 p.m. Write a line in the journal. Nothing profound. *Just a line.* Then lie on the couch. Stare at the ceiling. The house is quiet, except for the fridge humming in the kitchen.

March 18

3:15 a.m. Wake up. Sip water. Stare at the wall. The day runs through my head like a train that doesn't stop.

6:00 a.m. Open *Moby-Dick*. Try to read at least 10 pages. Stare at the sentence: "the whiteness of the whale." Close the book. Shower. Let the water go cold and think about how long it takes to die of hypothermia.

10:00 a.m. Oncology rounds. Mr. Vassilis, still cracking jokes, asks, "Do I look good enough to get discharged?" I tell him he does. He grins like he believes me. Mrs. Garbis coughs the entire time I'm with her. The sound makes my stomach turn.

12:15 p.m. Lunch. A meeting disguised as networking. I nod a lot, but I'm not listening. All I can think about is how to adjust Mr. Vassilis's pain meds without making him a zombie.

3:00 p.m. Back at the clinic. Charts. Notes. Click. Type. Blink. The clock moves slower than I do.

6:30 p.m. Dinner. Briam. Too salty. Too bland. I finish it anyway. Stare at the plate for ten minutes, then throw it in the sink.

9:30 p.m. Write in the journal again. Just one line: *Today was a day*. Close it. Open my inbox. Reply to two emails. Ignore the rest. Sign off with "Best."

March 25

6:00 a.m. Shower. Rehearse the day's tasks. Say their names in order: Kallistratou. Damianou. Vassilis. Pavlina. Filippou. Water goes cold. I don't turn it off.

8:30 a.m. First patient. A man in his fifties with a bad knee. Tells me he got it playing soccer in his twenties. "Think I'll ever play again?" he asks, grinning. I tell him no without saying no. He nods like he already knew.

3:45 p.m. Home visits. Mrs. Pavlina is at the stove again, stirring her stew. I tell her to stop. She ignores me. "Eat more," she says, handing me a bowl. I do. She smiles like it's a victory. Mr. Filippou's in a bad mood. Complains about the neighbor's dog barking all night. His tea's already made, but his hands are shaking too much to pour it.

6:30 p.m. Dinner. A microwaved casserole that tastes like cardboard. Chew slowly. Think about Mrs. Garbis coughing. Think about the blood pressure cuff. Don't touch it.

8:00 p.m. Lie on the floor. Stare at the ceiling. Try to feel small. It doesn't work.

9:00 p.m. Write one more line: *I don't know if I'm helping anyone.* Close it. Shut off the lights. Lie in bed. Wait for the next day.

"That's not a planner," I said, looking at the entries. "This is a diary. I mean this is something…literary." I couldn't find my name anywhere, but he let me see only old entries. I wanted to flip through the pages, but I didn't dare.

Pappi took it from my hands and put it back in his backpack.

"This keeps me focused," he said, almost defensive. "Helps me keep it together." He paused—just long enough for me to catch it. "Why don't you try it? Write about your accident. Start there."

The way he said it—calm, casual, like it was nothing—made me want to laugh. Or throw something. Or maybe just disappear.

But me and the accident? Yeah, it was time we had a chat.

"God, it's really hot," I told the person next to me at the bar. "I think they intentionally want to make it as steamy as possible so that we drink more."

He smiled at me, raised his cup, and gestured with cheers.

"Seems like it's working."

I drank the vodka and Red Bull and popped an ecstasy pill. I didn't remember who I had come with. At this point, I was alone. There were a few people I knew, but none of them were from my original circle. I felt like one of those creeps, going out by themselves, circling the place for young girls. There was an invisible audience in my head, laughing at me for being here by myself. For not having friends. For being desperate enough to show up alone. I remembered when I was younger, much younger, and went to some shitty high school discotheque. Same story. No one to go with. Just me and a bottle of vodka I hid in my bra upon entering. I saw a few kids from school and walked over, holding out the bottle like it was a peace offering. They looked at me like I was something vile, as if I had some incurable disease that spread through the air. Then they glanced at each other like they shared some secret information about me I was not let in on. Everything was going to be great soon, and I would forget all this nonsense.

The thing was that it didn't kick in as it was supposed to—the pill. I got really paranoid and clenched my jaw. For some reason, I couldn't stop thinking about the past. It just wouldn't leave me alone. Of cours, I did the worst possible thing I could do. I decided to leave and go home, realizing I was still high out of my eyeballs. I knew my parents were there, but I didn't care; I just wanted to get out of here. The worst decision was not that. The worst decision was that I chose to drive.

It was pouring and in my head played that Prince Song, "Purple rain, purple rain". I grabbed my phone at a stoplight—fingers slick and fumbling—and opened YouTube. The wheel felt wrong in my hands. I shouldn't be holding it. The rain slammed down harder. I found the song—Prince, a concert video, him in that suit with the ruffles—and I sang along, humming the words. The contrast with the electronic music I'd just heard at the club hit me with a nice, intense feeling.

The darkness blurred the edges of the city, and the lights scattered below looked like distant stars, as if the whole place had been lifted off the ground and set adrift in space. Everything felt suspended, half-real; like it could dissolve at any moment. I thought about driving through the stars, slipping past the last traces of home, moving forward into the endless dark. Time changed in space, didn't it? Dilated or collapsed. Maybe it didn't matter. Maybe we'd adjust, the way we always did, until the strange became familiar, until we forgot it had ever been different at all.

Then my phone rang.

The crash happened in an instant. One second everything was fine, and the next—I saw myself lying next to the car, right by the tire. So peaceful, like a sleeping dog. The warmth leaking out of me, floating into the cold air.

Then it was dark. I was awake, or at least I thought I was, but I couldn't open my eyes. Something was off. I didn't know where I was, but my gut told me something had gone very wrong. I tried to hold on to the feeling, to trace it back to the moment before the crash, but I couldn't. I was out before the ambulance even arrived.

I drifted, slipping in and out of consciousness. I remembered a sci-fi book I'd read once—about a guy who woke up just like this, groggy and confused, only to realize he was on a spaceship. They'd put him into an artificial coma to make him miss the long trip from Earth to another galaxy. I liked that idea.

I fantasized for a moment, imagining I was that guy. Maybe my brain had been catatonic this whole time, and this was it—my awakening. Maybe I was doing something important for NASA, and when I opened my eyes, I'd see the stars waiting for me. 31.12.2022, Happy Fucking New Year, Ayla.

07: AFTER THE WRECK, I PICKED MYSELF UP, SPREAD MY WINGS, AND FLEW AWAY

Now I found myself waiting for Pappi. Before, not long ago, it had been the doctors—my life reduced to rounds, appointments, questions. Now Pappi. His face was the one I saw most often during my last days at the hospital. I still couldn't take that name seriously.

One afternoon, as sunlight streaked across the room, Pappi asked, "Where do you think you'll be a year from now?"

I didn't answer at first. *Would I be with Selen?* The thought curled around me.

"Alive, probably," I said. "The bar's that low."

"Come on," he said. "Humor me."

"Does anybody know where they'll be in a year?"

"Well, yes," he said, as though the answer were obvious.

"You can lie to yourself if it makes you feel better."

And then he did something strange. He laughed. A short, quiet laugh, like he didn't mean to let it out.

"You're going full *carpe diem*, then?" he said. "That's your plan?"

"Most certainly."

"Look where it got you."

I wanted to say something sharp, something that would cut. But the words wouldn't come.

"So you think you know the answer to your question?" I asked him.

"Oh, yes. Absolutely." And then he added, handing me the resistance band, "Let's play a game."

I took the band, tugging it between my hands, testing the resistance like I always did.

"What kind of game?"

"A prediction game. Just for fun. Where will you be in a year or five years? Where will the world be?"

"And what happens if I don't play?"

He leaned back, smirking like some smug oracle. "But, Ayla, you already are."

I rolled my eyes. "You think you're so clever. Fine, let's play your game. Mass euphoria," I said, hooking the resistance band under one foot and pulling it taut, the stretch burning through my arms and shoulders.

"Not the good kind, though. I mean *Brave New World* euphoria. Everyone's happy because they've been drugged into submission."

His eyebrows went up.

"You've read *Brave New World*?"

"I read, yes. Don't be condescending."

"Well, look at you," he said, with the tone of someone patting a dog that learned a new trick.

I ignored him, pressing my foot harder into the band. "Prescriptions for kids who can't focus because their parents handed them a tablet when they were two. Entire societies running on drugs—study enhancers, pills for kids, capsules for workers to make the grind more grindable. I'm talking anger dressed up as joy, alienation packaged as connection."

"Bleak," he said.

"Accurate."

He saw progress. I saw apocalypse.

In my mind, algorithms would replace employees—and fire them. Society would fracture into thousands of little sects, controlled by an algorithmic government more than by free will. *Wait, what free will?* Politics was as distant to me as a cloud in the sky—my private fuck you to my father, but I had strong opinions about the mind and consciousness. Even the body, which was entirely Pappi's domain.

He told me to let go of the band, and his hands moved to my ankle, rotating it gently, testing the joint. The rhythm of his movements had become familiar—press, rotate, release, repeat. There was a sudden tug as he adjusted my position.

"Fragmentation," I said, exhaling as he flexed my foot forward.

"Decentralization," he countered, steadying my leg as he bent it at the knee.

"Don't sugarcoat it."

"Why not? You think the future's a conspiracy theory waiting to happen?"

"Yes, absolutely."

That shut him up, briefly. He propped my leg on his shoulder, kneeling slightly as he worked into the tension in my hamstring. His thumbs pressed into the muscle, deliberate and slow, and I couldn't help the hiss of air that escaped my teeth.

"You're wrong," he said finally, pushing deeper into the stretch.

"Prove it."

"I don't have to," he said, stepping back. "The kids will do it for me."

"What kids?"

"The ones running barefoot through fields."

I groaned. "Please kill me now. That is so lame! There won't be fields."

"There will," he said, crouching to check my alignment.

"There won't."

"We'll be going backwards," he said, lightly tapping my knee as a cue to keep it straight. "In a good way. Kids reclaiming childhood. Families turning off the Wi-Fi. Schools banning phones—"

"Now you're just fantasizing," I said, gritting my teeth as I switched legs. "You think we're headed for some pastoral utopia?"

"Not utopia," he said, pressing deeper into the pose. "Balance—"

"Oh, come on," I interrupted. "You really think people are gonna give all this up? The dopamine, the instant gratification? Look, I'm not a visionary, okay? I can't think beyond this... this state I'm in." I gestured vaguely to the hospital room around me. "But I know one thing. Families? Gone. Marriage? Dead."

"Interesting," he said. "You're calling the death of love, then?"

I didn't answer right away, but I stopped mid-movement.

"You're so dramatic. Or is it romantic? They just don't work, Pap. No family units anymore. People will figure that out eventually. There'll be estrangement—generations barely speaking. Dogs at home with more soul than humans. Cats replacing brothers. You think I'm wrong?"

"Maybe, and please don't call me Pap," he said. "Maybe not. Predicting the future is more about what's happening now than truly predicting the future."

"You're OK with Pappi, but Pap's too much?" I said and frowned. "So, I'm... projecting."

"All the time. As am I."

"Well, do you believe in families, then? Marriage? Or are you—"

"What? Married?" He snickered. "No. Not married. Family, though? Maybe. Someday."

"You said that you knew?" I asked, shifting on the bed, the ache from earlier still lingering in my muscles.

"Knew what?" Pappi replied.

"Where you'll be one year from now."

"Yes," he said, watching me with that same infuriating calm.

"And?"

"A year from now, I'll be living in a cave," he said. His voice was steady as if he was announcing tomorrow's weather.

I stared at him. And then I laughed—hard. The sound burst out of me. "You can't be serious," I said.

"You don't believe me?"

"I don't," I said firmly, shaking my head for emphasis.

"You'll see," he said, standing to stretch his arms above his head, as if his own muscles needed some relief now.

I expected everything else but this answer. Was Pappi a liar, like me? This excited me.

He rolled his shoulders and grabbed the resistance band from the table, tossing it into a basket by the door. "That's enough for today," he said casually, completely ignoring how the conversation had just spiraled into something strange and unpredictable.

I walked, and I walked with zero help. My crutches clattered against the hospital hallway, my arms shook, my ribs screamed. I walked, and I hated walking. I walked, and I loved it, too, because each step was proof that I was real. That I was still alive.

At the same time, I was conscious this meant the end of my time with Pappi. I could feel it slipping away minute by minute; sand pooling at the bottom of an hourglass.

There was a bug in my brain. A suspicion.

I should have been discharged a while ago. Pappi had once let it slip that I could have gone home even before I could walk. But I hadn't pressed him on it. I didn't want the answer. My suspicion? My father. He'd always been a man who believed in consequences, and he was itching to teach me a lesson. Maybe he was punishing me, keeping me here to stew in my mistakes for one extra month.

What my father didn't know was that I didn't mind. I preferred to stay here and leave the hospital in the best possible shape, instead of recovering at home. The joke was on him. He thought he was keeping me trapped. Let him waste his money—every extra day in this private prison was a day I didn't have to spend at home. I had Pappi here. And I had time to plan how I'd find my ghost of a sister; how I'd pull her back from wherever she'd gone.

Sometimes that hopefulness easily gave way to panic. Because outside, there was nothing. No Pappi. No sister. Nothing but the wreckage of my life waiting to swallow me up again. Would Pappi follow me into the outside world? Or would he leave like everyone else?

I had his number, saved for scheduling our sessions, but the thought of using it outside these walls made my stomach twist. Would he even answer if I called? Or was I just another patient to him, another broken person on a long list of others he needed to fix? His number and my parents' were the only ones stored in the basic, non-smart phone I'd been given—no apps, no internet, no distractions.

I had spent a total of 97 days in the hospital. Three months and seven days. And on my last day here I waited for him in the small hospital gym, the big mirror on the wall reflecting me back to myself. One crutch. One twisted body. One desperate girl pretending not to be desperate.

"So, this is it," I said.

Pappi looked up from the chart he was writing in. "What's it?"

"My last session," I said, forcing a smile. "The last time you get to boss me around."

He laughed, but it sounded distracted.

"Don't sound so excited," I said. "You'll miss me, you know."

"Of course," he said, glancing at me briefly before returning to the chart.

I hated how casual he was, like this didn't matter at all.

"Pappi," I said, and his name came out sharp, like a hook.

"What's up?"

"I was thinking..." I hesitated. "You've been a big part of my recovery. I wouldn't have made it this far without you."

"I'm just doing my job," he said.

"But it's more than that," I added, "—for me, at least."

He didn't say anything, and I pressed on.

"I want to keep going," I said. "The progress. The work. And whatever this is..." I lifted a hand, motioning between us. "I don't want to lose that."

"Ayla—"

"Not as my physiotherapist," I said quickly. "Just... as you."

He hesitated, and I could see the wheels turning in his head.

"I don't know if that's a good idea," he said finally.

"Why not?" I asked, letting my voice drop. "You've said it yourself—you want to get out of this place. See the world. Live in a cave, for fuck's sake. I do too. Maybe... maybe we could help each other."

He stared at me, and I thought I'd pushed too far.

And then he said, "Okay."

Just that. Just *okay*.

"Okay what?" I pressed.

"I was waiting for you to get better, and then to move on," he added, his voice flat, matter-of-fact. "You saw my calendar." A beat passed, and then, almost as an afterthought, "I want to leave. The hospital, the field—everything."

"Why did you even start working here?" I asked.

He shrugged, almost dismissively. "I'm close with your doctor. He's like a father to me. A friend, too. He mapped this whole path out for me—told me I could do good here. I guess I believed him."

"You know, it was me and him when you came in." Pappi continued. "He didn't think you'd make it. We actually made a bet on it."

I stared at him. "A *bet*?"

"Don't look so shocked. We are all cynics here. And he does that a lot. I think it's his way of managing his expectations. Doctors are funny like that."

"Ha ha," I replied.

There was something uncomfortably casual about the way he said it, just another detail in a long list of things I wasn't supposed to take personally. *Was I not a person?*

"What will you do?" I asked, changing the subject before I could let it settle too deeply. And then added, "Besides the cave."

He leaned back, as if considering the question for the first time. "Don't know yet. Maybe live in nature. Maybe try the whole work-nomad thing—travel the globe, see what happens." He looked at me, as though assessing my stamina for the conversation. "So don't waste my time. Let's get this over with."

"Pappi," I said suddenly, catching his gaze. "Did you know I heard your voice?"

He blinked, confused. "Sorry?"

"I think... I think when I was brought in, I heard your voice. You said I wasn't dead yet. Not yet. I held on to those words. Your words took me out of the coffin."

He didn't respond at first, just looked at me, his expression unreadable.

Then, finally, he said, "I remember."

I waited, but nothing else came. No explanation, no deeper acknowledgment. Just those two words.

Something about that should've made me angry, but it didn't. Maybe because I understood. This wasn't the place for anything more.

Pappi glanced down at his chart, pen tapping once against the paper. "Come on," he said. "Let's wrap this up."

I didn't argue.

St. Luke's finally sent me away, but not empty-handed. No, the hospital gave me a parting gift—a discharge summary, neatly typed, listing everything the crash had shattered and what they'd done to piece me back together.

- **CONTUSIO THORACIS** – Contusion of the chest (hurt less than being called a swine by my father—or worse.)

- **HYDROPNEUMOTHORAX BILATERALIS** – Bilateral hydropneumothorax (lungs crushed, but I've known worse pressure—words, hands, silence, all pressing down and pressing in.)
- **RETROPERITONEUM ET SCARIFICATIO ABDOMINALIS** – Injury involving the abdominal cavity (an open wound, but nothing new. I've been bleeding for years.)
- **HAEMOPERITONEUM** – Presence of blood in the abdominal cavity (as if I hadn't already spilled enough—on floors, on sheets, on nights I don't talk about.)
- **RUPTURA LIENIS** – Rupture of the spleen. (something inside me burst, but wasn't it always like this? Things breaking? Soft things break. Left unrepaired.)
- **STATUS POST THORACOSTOMIAM** – Status post-thoracostomy (they cut me open so I could breathe. No one thought to ask why I'd been suffocating.)
- **STATUS POST LAPAROTOMIAM ET SPLENECTOMIAM** – Status post-laparotomy and splenectomy (stitched back together, held up by thread and hope. One of those won't last.)
- **FRACTURA FEMORIS MULTIPLEX** – Multiple fractures of the femur (a shattered leg, but I was broken long before this—bones heal, other things don't.)

In the hospital, I was pretty isolated, so I still hadn't grasped the entirety of my own predicament, and especially my sister's disappearance. There were posters of her. I didn't even realize she was missing, as in police-looking-for-her missing. As in vanished-into-the-darkness-of-the-world missing. I was protected by all that, tucked away inside the sterile walls of my hospital room.

But now, in the blank space where my life was supposed to continue, the cocoon was gone. All I had was her absence. And Pappi's, too.

He didn't answer my texts anymore. I sent one yesterday morning: *Hey, how's it going? Raising any invalids from the dead today?* I stared at the screen for a few minutes after sending it. It felt light, harmless, even funny. The kind of message someone normal would send. No response. Then another, an hour later: *Seriously, Pappi, how are you? What's new in the world of miracles?* By the end of the day, I'd sent four, and by midnight, I hated myself for all of them.

The silence was unbearable. I imagined him looking at his phone, seeing my name pop up again, and sighing, maybe even rolling his eyes. He was the one person I still felt tethered to, and now that tether was unraveling, thread by thread.

I hadn't told anyone about Pappi. About how much I'd come to rely on him in the hospital. He was supposed to be temporary—just one of the many interchangeable faces that passed through my room, clipboard in hand, asking me to rate my pain or try another exercise. But, somehow, he wasn't interchangeable. Somehow, he stayed.

And now he wasn't answering my texts. Was I overreacting? I caught myself imagining things: him showing up, standing at my door. The wild relief in his eyes, like he finally understood something about me, something important.

The house felt too large. Too empty. The kind of space that should hum with life, but instead hung heavy with its absence. I wandered the hallways with no real purpose, the soles of my feet sliding across cold, veined marble, polished to a blinding sheen.

There was bread on the counter. I opened the fridge and took out the butter and a half-empty carton of milk. I didn't feel hungry, but I put two slices of bread in the toaster anyway. As I waited, I looked out the window. It was raining, but just barely, the typical April rain that looked like mist settling over the street. The view through the big window was breathtaking. Thessaloniki lay stretched out like a vast body, its edges blurred by the sea. When the toast popped up, I let it sit there too long and it turned cold. I ate it standing at the counter, staring at the rain, and took a large sip of milk straight from the carton.

I walked back into the living room. A poster lay on the kitchen table, face down. I didn't flip it over. I knew what it said. Instead, I sat in the armchair by the window. The rain was steady now, tapping softly against the glass. I closed my eyes and leaned my head back. In the darkness behind my eyelids, I could almost hear her laugh.

There were mirrors here, everywhere—framed in ornate gold, standing tall in corners like silent sentries. My reflection slipped in and out as I walked, pale and indistinct, like a ghost that didn't quite belong. I came to a room that must have been hers. The door was ajar, just enough to show me a sliver. For a long moment, I stood there, staring at the narrow crack of light.

Inside, the room was almost untouched. There was a bed, neatly made, with white linens that looked like they had never been slept in. A dressing table sat against the wall, its surface scattered with small, intimate things—lip balm, a hairbrush with strands of light blonde hair still caught in its teeth, a ring resting on its side. I reached for the brush without thinking, my hand hovering above it for a second, as if it might burn me if I touched it. I ripped the blonde hairs from its bristles and held them in my palm.

The hair. Her hair. I'd seen it in the photo. Long, almost white in the sun, curling slightly at the ends. It was the only part of her I could picture, the only piece of her that felt real. And here it was, caught in the teeth of a cheap plastic hairbrush, a detail so mundane it made my chest ache.

I looked at the shelves—books lined up perfectly, alphabetized. A pair of running shoes neatly placed beneath the bed, as though she might slip them on at any moment and jog back into the world.

There was a mirror over the dresser, rimmed with white fairy lights. I leaned in, my breath fogging the glass. Red hair, messy and too long now, clinging to my neck like something I'd forgotten to cut off. I looked tired. Not just tired—worn down, used up, like life had chewed me up and spit me out. I traced my finger down the reflection of my jaw, but it wasn't delicate and feminine. Nothing about me was. The girl in the mirror didn't belong here, in this room with its neat little touches and ghostly lavender scent. She belonged somewhere dirtier, somewhere where people didn't expect her to smile.

Selen's clothes were folded into perfect rectangles. A clean scent lingered, not just lavender, but something familiar, yet just out of reach. My fingers brushed the sleeve of a cashmere sweater, and something tightened in my throat. I hadn't expected this. My mother had been here; left her touch. I recognized her style. I could feel her presence in the careful arrangement, the color choices. Or was my sister a basic bitch? The messy brush, strands of her hair still tangled in it, gave me hope that she wasn't. I wondered why my mother had left them there. Had she simply not seen them? No, my mother wasn't the type to overlook things like that. Maybe it was too painful to rip them away.

I sank into the edge of the bed, the mattress barely shifting beneath my weight. The rain outside had picked up, beating steadily against the windows now, but the sound was muffled by the thick curtains. The room felt alive and dead all at once. I thought of Pappi. Of the hospital. The way he would hold out a hand to help me, his voice calm and firm as he told me to take another step, to breathe, to push. I thought of the texts I sent him, his silence, the sense of falling into a void where no one would catch me. My hands rested in my lap, motionless, with Selen's hair in my fist.

I kept searching, moving through the space until my hand bumped into something hidden under a neat pile of towels in the closet. Paper. Folded, pressed flat. I pulled it out, smoothing it open. A sketch. Another underneath. The drawings stared back at me—eyes everywhere, uneven and wild. Some swollen and dark, others cutting into me, judging or begging. They spilled across faces that didn't fully exist, some of them half-formed, unfinished, like they had been started and abandoned.

My hand trembled as I folded the drawings again. Even hidden, the eyes followed me, unblinking.

08: GONE GIRL

The plan: First, I had to get out of the house. That was obvious. You didn't launch an investigation while sitting under your parents' roof, their eyes watching you like some glass figurine on the verge of cracking. Thessaloniki's glossy Panorama neighborhood wasn't the right place for me; its streets were polished and bright, designed to display the perfect versions of people, not the messy truths underneath.

I went back to the dorms in town. Not because I wanted to reconnect with other students or rehabilitate my GPA—God, no. The thought of classes, of sitting in a lecture hall pretending to care about anything other than Selen made me sick. But the university wasn't home. It gave me freedom. Distance. A reason not to answer my parents' questions.

Pappi still hadn't answered my texts. Seven days now. A whole week. Today, I'd call him. Or I'd try.

Without my phone (the police still had it), I asked my mother for numbers. She had two: Anna, my childhood friend, and Eleni, the daughter of one of her friends—whose name alone made me wince. My mother always said I should spend more time with her. She still didn't seem to understand that Eleni was a mean cunt.

I messaged Anna.

Me: *Hey, it's Ayla. Back from the dead. Do you have a minute? Need to ask you something.*

Her: *Whoa, you're alive! Where have you been?*

Me: *Not in the mood for small talk. This is about my sister.*

Her: *Oh.*

Me: *Let's meet up?*

Her: *Call me in two hours.*

The conversation fizzled after that.

Back at the dorm, I felt like my story hung in the air, stamped across my face. I was born. My parents had money. I went to school. I fucked for the first time, whatever age that was. Then came the college years, the endless blur: a hundred men, a hundred nights, sex for love, sex for hate, transactional sex, empty sex, sex that scorched my insides until I couldn't tell if it was pleasure or rage anymore. Anal. Oral. Drugs. Drinking. Petty theft. Shitty friends. Getting dumped over and over. There was a rhythm to it, the rise and fall of a tide I couldn't control.

Then the crash. My body ripped apart, nearly dead, barely stitched back together. Limping now, propped up by a crutch, dragging myself back here—too close to my parents, too far from my sister.

Selen.

Where were you?

What struck me as strange was how kind everyone was; their smiles were stiff, puppet-like, as if their strings had been pulled too hard. Concern rippled through them like a reflex, rehearsed and unnatural. *What happened?* they asked, their voices climbing, their brows pitched in perfect concern. Girls, guys—it was all the same, a script performed flawlessly.

"Oh, I'm okay," I told them. "It wasn't that serious. I just needed a little vacation afterward." A neat answer, simple, digestible. It let them smile and move on, satisfied. They didn't want the truth. Or if they wanted it, it wasn't for the right reasons.

"It wasn't serious? We heard you were in the hospital."

"Only for a couple of days, never lost consciousness."

My first instinct was concealment, and I went with it. People had called me a pathological liar so many times, I'd stopped bothering to deny it. But for all my secrets, I was still the kind of person who thrived on attention—I was the kind who craved it, even as I twisted every story I told. It was partly the reason I lied so much: to amuse and bemuse my audience. Now I was quieter. That was the only thing that changed. My values hadn't been reformed, nor my morals.

I think that was partly Pappi's influence too. He was a very private person, and I had the habit of latching on to people, absorbing their personalities onto mine.

My new roommates were two Kazakhstani girls who looked at me as though I was the plague embodied. I was glad I had roommates who weren't popular, who had zero interest in me, and who, most likely, wouldn't speak to me unless absolutely necessary.

Ashley and Monica were long gone now. But absence didn't erase what came before. They still lingered—not in the air, not in the halls, but in the way my stomach clenched at certain songs, in the way my fingers hesitated before opening my phone, in the way laughter that wasn't theirs still made my chest tighten. Phantom pain, Laskaris would call it. The body remembering something it no longer had. The heart doing the same.

"I have decided on something important," I told Anna. "Can I see you and talk to you about Selen?"

"Can't you say it over the phone?"

"I don't think I can."

"Okay, I'll let you know when that can happen."

There was someone else who also wanted to discuss Selen: the police.

"Maybe she wanted to start a new life," the older detective kept saying. "Did she go out a lot? Did she have a lot of boyfriends?" He looked like a man in his forties, but he also could have been in his fifties. He had one of those faces. A strong mustache covered his lip, and it made him look like a balding porn actor. He was a firm four. The young detective had yet to speak. I hadn't heard his voice. He was a potential for a seven.

"As you know, I don't remember Selen. I can only tell you if she had a lot of boyfriends if I hear it from someone else, and I haven't." I was sick of their questions. "There was a doctor—no, a psychologist—in the hospital responsible for my psychological assessment. Have you talked to her?"

Little did I realize that my problems with this institution had just begun.

The cops wanted to punish me. Driving drunk, high as a kite, my car wrapped around a lamppost, crushed like a can. These things didn't just disappear. They looked at me like I was scum, like just another spoiled little shit who thought the rules didn't apply. They didn't care about my injuries. About my pain. They cared only that I'd broken the law.

My father stepped in. And with him came Eliezer Levi. Levi wasn't what I expected. I had heard my father speak of him many times, but never met the man. He looked more like an overfed accountant than a lawyer—balding, soft around the edges, a face that creased up like he'd spent years smiling at family dinners. But, as I quickly found out, that was just the packaging.

"First rule," he said, pointing a stubby finger at me the day before our court appearance, "you're going to look like the kind of girl they *want* to forgive." He gave me a wardrobe rundown like he was dressing me for Sunday school. No makeup, clean hair pulled back, minimal jewelry. Neat. Respectable. Innocent. He didn't trust me to pull off "remorseful," so he settled for "harmless." I looked like a smart fox dressed as a straight-A student. I admit, it made me laugh. He even put a tie on me.

The laughter died fast.

Five years. That was what I was looking at. Five years behind bars, a felony conviction stamped onto my name, my life rearranged into something I wouldn't recognize by the time I got out. Did Greek prisons even have those orange jumpsuits, or was that just in movies?

"She nearly died," Levi kept saying. The way he told it, my broken body was punishment enough, and the court didn't need to add to it.

We worked out a deal, though. I pled guilty, admitted to reckless driving under the influence. In exchange, I got a suspended sentence. Three years. If I so much as breathed wrong, I'd be locked away for all of them.

My license was revoked for five years. I had six months to pay €30,000. I was required to provide biological samples to the police for toxicology monitoring. I was also ordered to attend mandatory rehabilitative counseling sessions with a court-appointed psychologist for the duration of my suspension period. It was all still crashing down, but it wasn't five years in a cell.

They let me keep Laskaris as my appointed psychologist. Levi convinced the judge that switching therapists would disrupt my recovery.

The gavel came down.

Levi gave my shoulder a squeeze at the end. "You are aware of the severity of these charges?" he asked.

I nodded.

"It would be most advisable, my dear, to express your gratitude to your father with greater frequency," he went on.

I should have said something, some small, obedient word, but my mouth stayed shut. Gratitude. Yeah, sure.

"You dodged a bullet, Ayla," he whispered, smiling in that quiet way of his. But there was nothing lucky about it. He'd pulled the strings, I'd put on the act, and that was the end of it.

For now.

I met with Anna the day after the hearing. She shifted in her seat, fingers tapping lightly against her cup, her eyes darting around the café before landing back on me. "You want random memories?" she asked. "Fine. I remember Selen used to boss you around."

I hadn't told Anna the entire truth, of course. But she got what was closest to the truth: that my memories were a little scrambled from the accident, and that I was trying to remember if Selen had ever told me she wanted to escape—or if she even had a plan.

Anna and I had been friends since first grade. Our lives had always been intertwined. Even for that entire year we spent in the States, her family traveled with us. She was the one person whom I'd told versions closest to the truth. Did Selen receive the naked truth from me or did I hide myself from her like I did with the rest of the world?

Anna stirred her coffee absently, her spoon clinking against the ceramic mug in a steady rhythm. "Do you remember basketball camp? That summer before fifth grade?"

I frowned, trying to summon the memory. "Kind of. Why?"

Anna's lips curled into a faint smile, though there was something cautious about it, like she was testing the waters. "I still think about that prank Selen pulled. You don't remember?"

"Who got pranked?"

Anna looked right at me. "You, Ayla."

I held her stare, waiting for more.

She nodded. "Yeah. That summer, you followed Selen everywhere. She was with the older girls from her team, but she always had you trailing behind, like her little mascot. One afternoon, during free time, she and her friends decided to 'make you over.'"

Anna's eyes flicked to me, then back to her coffee. "They did your hair, teased it all big and wild, smeared on bright red lipstick, rouged up your cheeks. They even put one of their bras over your naked body. Then they shoved you outside and locked the door.

"I remember you banging on the door, yelling for her to let you in, but she didn't." Anna added gently. "So you stood there, outside, looking like a mini whore."

Anna's smile was faint, apologetic. "You came back inside eventually, red-faced, ready to kill her, and she just laughed and said, 'It's no big deal. You'll get over it.' And you did. By dinner, you were at her side again, like nothing had happened."

"She always got away with things?" I asked quietly.

"She did." Anna paused, her fingers tightening around her cup. "Just like you."

I looked down at my hands, my chest heavy. Anna spoke again.

"She would do something like that, but then she would also stick up for you. Do you remember that boy?" she asked. "We were in fifth grade maybe? What was his name? Niki, Nikolaos?"

"What of him?"

"He used to hang around the basketball courts after school."

"Yes, that fucker," I said. He was such an ass.

Anna was a witness to my demise in school. She was a bystander to the constant bullying and name-calling. I was not ashamed in front of her.

She leaned closer, her voice dropping as if she were sharing something too raw to say aloud. "One time he grabbed you. I remember it. You were so upset, crying your eyes out. You didn't even have the words to explain what he did, but everyone saw it. He did it at the basketball court, right there in front of everyone."

I stared at her, my hands tightening around the edge of my chair. The memory flickered faintly at the edges of my mind. How he crushed my small tits, trying to stick his hand in my jeans.

"And Selen—she found out." Anna's tone softened. "She didn't just let it go, you know. She got her friends involved—older kids, mostly boys. They cornered him after school in the alley behind the gym."

Anna paused, her eyes flicking over me before continuing.

"They beat the crap out of him. I heard they made him eat cigarette butts. Made him kneel every time he saw you after that. He had to apologize over and over. You were ecstatic." Anna's lips curled into a faint, humorless smile. "I think she became your hero then."

"You remember?"

No.

"Maybe. Now that you mention it."

Anna leaned back, exhaling victoriously, her gaze dropping to the table. "That was your dynamic. She'd mess with you, push you to the edge—but if anyone else dared to touch you..." She trailed off, shaking her head as if words couldn't capture it. "You were her little sister. That's what it meant."

Silence stretched between us, thick and uncomfortable. I searched for something to say, something that wouldn't feel like a lie. "Do you remember a place we used to hang out?"

Anna's eyes flicked back to mine, her expression unreadable. "The beach. That was your spot. Everyone knew we'd find you there—Selen dragging you into the water, you screaming about jellyfish."

She paused, her lips pressing into a thin line. "You know what? Also... the water tower."

I forced my face to stay neutral, my voice steady. "The water tower?"

"The one outside Thessaloniki, in Kallipoli. Do you remember that?"

Would she stop asking me if I remembered.

Anna leaned forward, her eyes narrowing as if trying to gauge my reaction. "You and Selen used to go there all the time. Sometimes you hitched a ride to get there. It was your thing, to think of different ways to get to the same place."

"I think I remember," I said quietly, though the words felt foreign in my mouth. I knew the place. But I had no memory of it being our place.

"You're sure? Because you'd better. That place... you two wouldn't shut up about it."

The water tower. Her words felt like a thread pulling loose from a fabric I'd kept tightly woven. The tower was ours, mine and Selen's, it seemed. A secret. I should have remembered more, but instead, all I felt was the weight of Anna's gaze, pressing against the fragile corners of my mind. Regardless, I knew the water tower. I knew where it was. And I remembered wondering what it might have been like to be born in that small village, in Kallipoli—a life boxed in by its limits. What it would have meant to live there, to stay there, to never escape. That was what my memories clung to.

Had I talked about this with Selen? No one but she could answer that.

Anna was still watching me, waiting for something. Maybe an answer. Maybe a reaction. I had nothing to give her.

"I should go," I said, pushing my chair back.

She didn't stop me.

I walked around without thinking, cutting through streets that felt too small, too known. The water tower lingered in my mind, but something else crept in, too. Pappi.

I thought of the way he spoke of his hometown, like a bad trick fate had played on him. "In my town, everyone killed boredom the same way—drinking, smoking weed, doing drugs. But not me. I read encyclopedias, won biology Olympiads, and studied. My parents and my teachers thought I'd make something of myself. An important politician. A doctor. But that was never my dream, only theirs." I knew he had told me that. I knew our connection was real.

But if I had grown up there, I wouldn't have been his friend. I would have been one of the kids who drank through the nights, burned through their days, let excess swallow them whole. The ones he left behind. And I felt it still—pulling at me, calling me back. The strange comfort of losing control.

I hit the clubs that weekend, though I calculated every sip of alcohol and snorted nothing. The police had me tagged now. Probation. Randomized checks. Breath tests. One misstep, one drink too many, and I was done. Prison was waiting, as I'd been reminded plenty.

In the club, the music pounded through me, bass lines vibrating in my chest. Some guy, shirt half-unbuttoned, eyes glossy, grabbed my crutch and started spinning it like a baton. Christ. What a dumb son of a bitch. A three, on a generous day.

"Hey, give it back!" I shouted, but my voice dissolved in the noise.

Before I could snatch it back, a tall blond man stepped between us, his shadow cutting through the neon haze. He said something I couldn't hear, and the thief faltered. A second later, the man handed me the crutch, his fingers brushing mine.

The eye candy was an eight.

"Thanks," I said, breathless. "I'm stupid. Shouldn't have come out. Want a drink?"

He nodded, following me to the bar.

"What happened?" he asked.

"Motorcycle accident."

"Oh," he said, "what about the driver?"

"Why'd you think I wasn't the driver? Because I'm a girl?" I slurped my cocktail, baiting him.

"Well, it's rare. Were you?"

"Yes," I said, grinning without humor. "But not a very good one. Obviously. The bike's gone now. Nothing but twisted metal and oil stains on the pavement."

"What bike was it?"

"Kawasaki."

"Sorry to hear that."

"You're sorry about the bike or about me?"

"You," he said, his voice thick with something close to pity. "I don't like motorcycles. I only asked out of politeness."

"Ever tried one?"

"No, and I don't intend to."

He said cheers. I said cheers. We drank. Too much. My calculations on how much alcohol I had in my system went to the shitter. By the time I brought him back to the dorm, my leg throbbed from the dance floor, a hollow ache I tried to ignore.

The room was dim, lit by the weak glow of a desk lamp. My two roommates were in their beds, one grunting as I stumbled in, the other pulling a pillow over her head.

He hesitated at the door, his face flushing. "Are they just going to—?"

"They don't care," I said, shrugging. But I caught the discomfort in his eyes, his reluctance to cross that line.

It didn't take long for the groping to start though—his hands clumsy, tugging at my shirt. Pain flared in my leg, sharp and insistent, but I shoved it down. The desire to fuck was stronger than the pain. At least, I told myself it was.

"Can we go to the bathroom?" he whispered.

"It will be difficult there for me," I said. But he insisted, and I pulled him toward it.

The fluorescent light flickered as we stepped in, buzzing like a trapped fly overhead. I reached for the switch on the wall.

"Don't," he said.

The door clicked shut behind us, and he locked it. He pressed me back against the sink, his breath on my neck, his fingers already pulling at the fabric between us.

"I want to see you," he murmured.

I hesitated, the light casting everything too bright, too raw.

When I pulled off my shirt, he froze, his eyes locking on the scar. It ran from my chest to my navel, a jagged, pale line the surgeons had stitched into me, like they'd tried to sew me back together with shaking hands. His fingers hovered over it, then traced it—slow and deliberate.

"That from the accident?"

"Yes."

He helped me take my jeans off. Up close, I noticed the deep-set lines of his skin. At the club, I thought he was younger—late twenties, maybe—but here, under the unforgiving bathroom light, his face shifted. His grin widened unnaturally, teeth too white, too big. Lashes, thick and dark, clumped together like they'd been dipped in ink. Something about him didn't look right.

His finger slid across my clit, rough and impatient, like he was tuning a busted radio. Too hard. Too fast. I caught his wrist, brought it to my mouth, and spat into his fingers. Then I guided him back, pressing his fingers down like I could teach him how to rub me. Didn't help. Still too pinchy. This was gonna be work.

His other hand traced the scar, his breath heavy against my neck. He pressed into me, fumbling with his jeans, unzipping his fly and pulling out his dick, movements jerky and uncoordinated. The body against mine twisted, his hips jutting forward. I was far from ready; plus the position hurt. Everything hurt.

His eyes kept darting to the mirror; he wanted to see himself, see me. His cock kept slipping out. He adjusted, grunted, tried again. His hands dug into my hips, but the angle was not right. What the hell was wrong with his eyelashes?

"You're tense," he muttered, annoyed, like it was my fault.

"Lick me," I said, cutting through his complaint, desperate to shift the dynamic. Desperate to feel something pleasant.

"I don't do that," he said flatly, pulling back just enough to look me in the eye.

"What?"

He ignored me.

Pain flared in my leg again. "We need to stop," I said, my voice trembling. "My leg hurts."

His gaze locked onto mine, sharp and unblinking, his face twisting into something harder to read. "You're not making any sense," he said, and his weight kept pressing me into the cold sink. Then, finally, he stepped back.

His hand returned to the scar, tracing it again, and I was suddenly too naked.

"What did it feel like?" he asked, as though the question wasn't strange at all. "When it happened."

I didn't answer. I didn't even understand what he meant.

His thumb slid along the uneven ridge, up to my chest. "Did they say you'd live? Or was it one of those... 'maybe she'll make it, maybe she won't' deals?"

"Why are you asking me this?" I tried to step back, but he didn't remove his hand.

"I'm curious," he said simply.

He zipped his jeans slowly, deliberately, his eyes never leaving mine. The look on his face was unreadable, like he was weighing something. His gaze flicked toward the door, still locked, then back to me.

Dread coiled tight inside me.

He chuckled and took a coin from his pocket. Let it rest between his fingers. A dull gleam under the fluorescent light.

"Heads or tails?" he asked.

"What?"

"Heads or tails? Choose."

"I should know what I'm calling."

"Just answer."

I exhaled. My hands curled against the sink. The porcelain cold against my skin.

"I'm not playing games with you."

"Then I'll play for you."

He flipped the coin. Caught it easily. Held it.

"One side we finish what we started," he said. "The other I walk out that door just like you want."

The bathroom was too small. The light too bright.

"I said I'm not playing."

Then he set the coin down on the sink beside me.

"You know what? You have two seconds before I scream. The girls in the next room aren't sleeping yet. And you're in a dorm."

He held onto the moment longer than he needed to. His hand lingered on the doorknob, his darting eyes daring me to move. Then, finally, he opened the door and left.

The slam echoed faintly behind him, leaving the room unbearably quiet.

I stayed there, gripping the edge of the sink, my chest heaving, heart pounding so loud I thought I might choke on it.

The gum in my mouth had melted, turning sour, sticky, sliding down my throat. What the fuck did I just dodge? Couldn't I just get a normal drunk you-suck-me-off-I-suck-you-off-let's-bang-byebye experience? Did I imagine all of it?

Was that how Selen disappeared? A one-night stand gone crazy.

The coin sat there. Waiting.

Heads.

I swallowed.

What would've happened if it had been tails?

The next day, I was still trying to shake the whole thing off. My class notes sat in front of me, my coffee growing cold beside them, but none of it was sinking in. Then the phone buzzed, slicing through the mess. Pappi.

"So?" I said.

"So what?"

"You disappeared."

"Had to sort my shit out."

"Yeah?"

"I quit the hospital."

"Jesus Christ. Did I break you?" I meant it to sound like a joke. It didn't.

"You give yourself too much credit."

"Could've said something. A text. A middle finger. Anything."

"I needed to end that first."

He was quiet for a moment. I could hear him breathing, hear the faint echo of street noise on his end of the line.

"I'll come see you," he said.

"Come here, then. Seen the college yet?"

A week later, Pappi stood in front of me like no time had passed. Same T-shirt, same crooked grin. I didn't say anything, just pulled him into a hug.

I jutted my leg out theatrically and knocked on it with my fist. "No more crutch for me," I said. "Tossed the damn thing."

Pappi snorted, eyeing my stance. "Yeah? And what does your leg think about that?"

"Doesn't get a say." I jerked my chin toward the car. "Get in."

I'd started driving again. A shitty green Opel Corsa I got off a guy who owed me. No papers, no bullshit. Just cash, a handshake, and me back behind the wheel where I wasn't supposed to be. Pappi slid into the back seat without a word, but I caught him watching me in the mirror.

"Why the back?" I asked.

"It's the safest spot," he said.

"You're weird."

"How the hell are you driving? Didn't they take your license?"

"They did."

"Aren't you afraid the police might stop you?"

"Not really. I've never been stopped by the cops while driving. Not once."

He didn't press it. Just unzipped his backpack, started digging around.

"You came by bus?" I asked.

"Yeah."

"Don't you have a car?"

"Don't you have better questions?"

I rolled my eyes. "You're older than me. Shouldn't you have your life figured out by now?"

"That's rich," he said. "Coming from you."

We hit a drive-thru, grabbed greasy gyros, and sat there eating in the car. The smell of fries hung heavy in the air, mixing with the faint, sour tang of gasoline. The sun beat down through the windshield, making the car feel even smaller.

Pappi was slouched in the back seat, pressed against the door. He ate slower than me—methodical, deliberate. Even his bites seemed planned. But he wasn't watching his food. He was watching *me*.

"The way you eat," he said, calmly. "It's like they've kept you hungry all your life."

He wasn't wrong. I wiped the grease from my fingers with a crumpled napkin.

"Never noticed that in the hospital," he added, his voice lower this time.

"Man, I was starving," I said, then grabbed the can of Mirinda from the seat next to me and pulled the ring. *Click-hiss.* I brought it to my lips, taking a long swig. The orange soda rushed down my throat, cold and fizzing, leaving a tangy bite.

Pappi shifted in the back seat. I could feel his eyes on me, but I didn't look up.

"Also," I added, "I love watching people eat with real zest. Truly going for it. Omnivores." The word stretching my mouth.

"There's a fetish like that," he said.

"Like what?"

"People who pay to watch an obese lady eat pancakes," he said, his tone even, almost thoughtful. "But some take it further. They don't just watch—they feed her. They make her bigger. Three hundred kilos. Four hundred. Until she can't move, can't turn over in bed, can't even lift her arms to take a bite herself. So they do it for her. Pancakes, burgers, shakes—whatever she wants, whatever she doesn't. That's the point. That's the kink."

"What a toxic interdependence," I said.

"It's so much worse for the woman," he said. "The men don't risk their bodies or their health. But the women... they die in agony."

I didn't know what to say to that. But I felt my guts twist.

"I had a patient like that once," he said after a moment. "She couldn't get out of bed by herself."

I put the gyro aside, having lost my appetite and gripped the steering wheel. Outside, the sun was relentless, glaring off the hood, making the asphalt shimmer.

"Eating disorders... they're a whole world of their own, aren't they?"

I didn't expect to say more, but the words rolled out of my mouth. "My mother sometimes pukes after meals. I don't know if it's a disorder or just a way to stay thin. For her, appearance is everything."

Fuck. Was that a lie? Did I just lie to Pappi? For a second, I wasn't sure. It was the truth. Wasn't it? It just had the polished edge of something practiced. Something I would say.

I flicked on the blinker and pulled onto the road. The car hummed beneath me, and before long, the open highway unfolded ahead.

"Where are we going?" Pappi asked finally, breaking the silence.

"You'll see," I said. "I'm taking us out of town."

He glanced at me, then out the window, watching the dry fields blur into the open sky. "Is this how I get kidnapped?"

"Yes, this is what happens to people who ignore my texts and calls for weeks."

I saw him smile, just a little.

"This whole Selen business has gotten pretty big." I said. "The police talked to me—asked me all sorts of questions. I've seen them with Laskaris a few times during my regular visits. Sometimes, one of them wants to sit in on our chats, but I can tell she really hates that."

"You still see her?"

"Yes. She's court-appointed now."

"How did that happen?"

"My lawyer. I'd already built a connection with Laskaris, so he made it work. She's got the right credentials—clinical psychology and whatever else the court wants. She's qualified. That's all they care about."

"Does she know that we are close?" he asked.

"Are we?" I asked back. "No. Also, I don't intend to tell her."

"It is so strange," I continued. "I still feel like it's one huge conspiracy where everyone is trying to convince me I have a sister when I don't."

"What do they say? Where is she? Any guesses?"

"You know that's the first time you've asked me." I said. "Nobody knows but they are looking at me like I do and like I am lying to them. Even my mother is always trying to extract nonexistent memories from me. You know she sends me pictures of her now and comes and hands me her clothes. She demands over the phone that I remember."

There was a pause in the car. We both looked at each other in the mirror. My first impression of him was incorrect. He actually looked sadder than usual, like a guy who had just lost a beloved, or someone extremely close. I couldn't put my finger on it exactly, but something had changed.

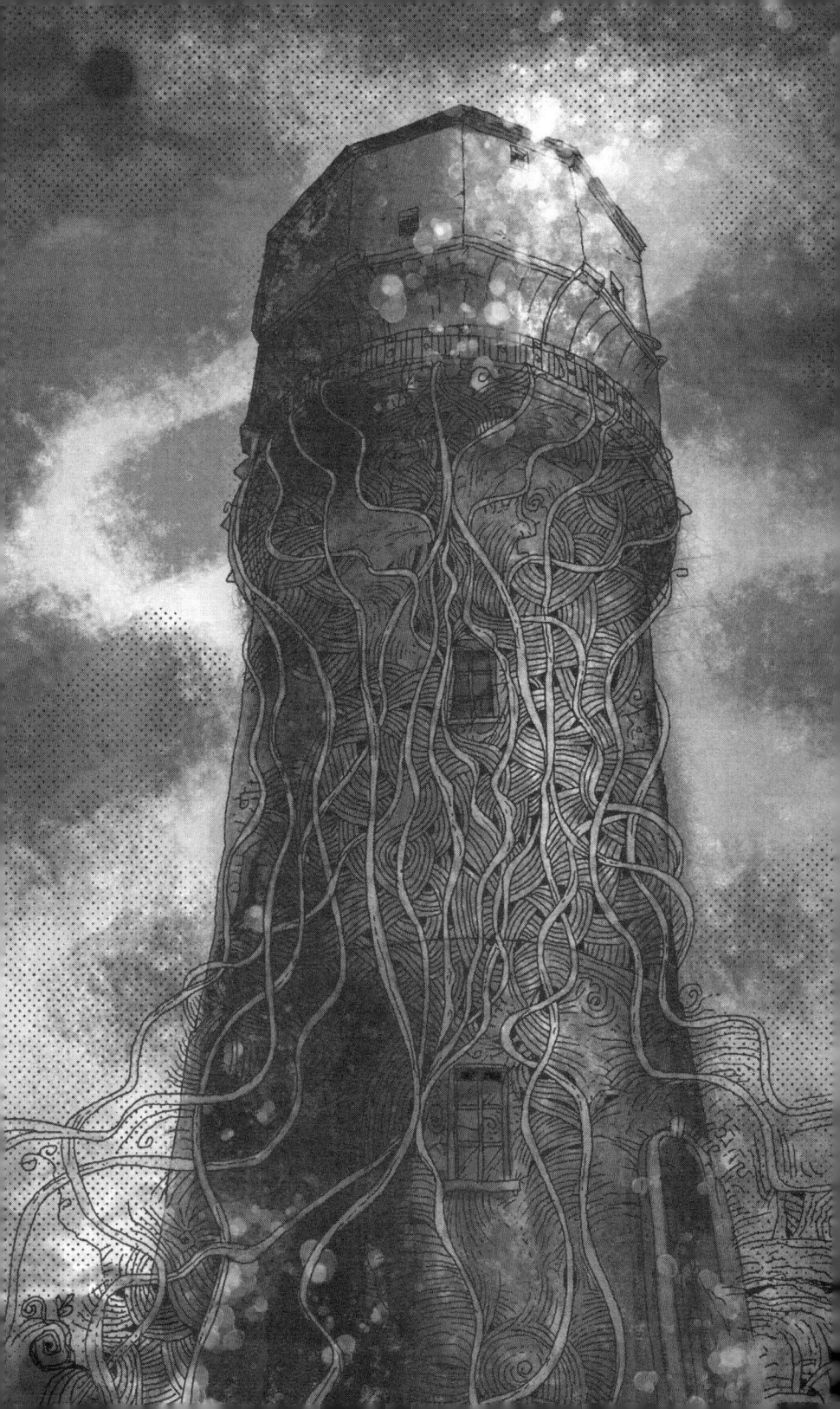

09: THE DARK TOWER

I pulled up and killed the engine. Pappi and I stepped out of the car.

The water tower stood like a spine in the flat landscape. The light was strong now, bleaching the sky to a pale, endless blue, with only a hint of gold lingering at the horizon.

"Have you ever been inside a water tower?" I asked.

"Can't say that I have."

"Well, that's what we're doing. This is the first clue to finding Selen."

Pappi turned to me, searching for something in my face. Whatever he was looking for, he must have found it. After a moment, he nodded.

The tower's slick metal surface rose in the half-light, streaked with ivy and rain, the kind of structure that seemed to belong more to the earth now than to us. Creeping ivy clawed up the sides of its sleek metal structure like the fingers of a patient hand. Beneath it, puddles had formed, spreading dark and still blotches of water.

We entered through the gate, Pappi right beside me.

"They don't lock this thing?" he asked.

"Well, what kind of crazy would want to go in?" I said.

Pappi just scoffed.

The door gave with a groan. Inside, the air was colder and heavy with dampness. Water dripped faintly somewhere above us, echoing down through the empty chamber.

We climbed.

The interior, stark and functional, was made gentler by the vines curling along the walls and the moss creeping over the floor. We walked through the cavernous space. The muted thrum of the bowels of the tower created a hum. The light filtered in through small windows, casting a diffused glow over the room. Dozens of narrow stairs wound upward in a tight, suffocating spiral. I moved through it like a swallowed thing caught inside a vast and indifferent body. The walls pressed in close, damp in places. Pappi shadowed me. I held up my phone, its weak glow barely cutting through the dark, but Pappi had a flashlight. Said he always kept one in his backpack. One of those guys who was always prepared.

"This place feels like it's waiting," I said, feeling the weight of the atmosphere pressing in on me. "Like it's holding its breath."

"Isn't it crazy…how we give everything human traits?" Pappi's voice cut through the quiet. Not so much an inquiry but a challenge. "Our need to humanize everything."

"I don't know. I really like it," I replied, my fingers trailing along the smooth metal walls. "It's like a dormant creature ready to come alive."

I found a concealed compartment, half-hidden by the shadow of a column. Inside, I found a collection of sketchbooks and paintbrushes, all meticulously arranged. A huge yellow eye stared out, painted on the wall. It looked too real. Whose eye was that? Selen's? I didn't think so. I'd seen the photos of her.

Moving to the next floor, we wandered into a large orbicular chamber where the whole wall was painted with eyes.

Every inch of the curved interior was covered in them—irises of every imaginable color, shape, and mood. There were eyes as pale as glaciers, their frozen blues fractured by the tiniest hints of yellow, like sunlight struggling to escape the ice. Others were deep, dark brown. Some were a muted green, raw and earthy, while others were like hazelnuts, glowing faintly, like dry autumn leaves caught in dim light.

The brushstrokes were precise, almost painfully so. You could see the microscopic details: the faint rings, the jagged bursts of pigment, the delicate spokes radiating from each pupil, as if the eyes were tiny suns. Some irises were flecked with faint white specks, catching the glow from Pappi's flashlight and trembling. Others had deep red undertones, but were not unrealistic.

And the pupils.

Some were wide, devouring the irises around them. Others were sharp pinpricks, tight with focus or fear. Together, they created an overwhelming sensation, a thousand gazes folding over you, stripping away any sense of safety or self.

The way they were painted... Some of the eyes stared straight at you, unblinking, almost defiant. Others were cast downward, as if shy or burdened, their lashes brushing the bottom edge of their frames. A few glanced sideways, wary, as though watching something—or someone—just beyond your reach. There were even eyes caught in mid-blink, half-lidded and wet with emotion.

The curvature of the tower made the experience even more disorienting. As I turned, the eyes seemed to shift their gaze, following me in eerie synchrony. The tower was alive, observing me as much as I was observing it.

And then, the texture of the wall: it was uneven, the paint layered so thick in some places it rose off the surface in ridges. In other places, the colors were faded, cracked, or peeling, as though the eyes themselves had grown exhausted from watching. The tower was a paradox—something ancient yet alive, something abandoned yet still brimming with intent.

We were surrounded.

Immersed.

For a moment, I could have sworn I heard it—the faint sound of a collective blink, a soft, whispered motion, lids closing in unison before opening again. Watching. Always watching.

Pappi shone the light on the biggest one. Then on the one next to it. Unlike the others, these two were different—they were part of a pair, connected, as if they belonged to the same face.

"Look familiar?" he asked.

"You think?"

"That's your heterochromia, yes."

There were my strange eyes, looking at me. Through her.

I wish it worked both ways.

"That's her. She painted these," I said, appreciating the intricacies of her designs.

"You think she knew it would resonate like this?" Pappi's voice held an edge of intrigue. "Or did she anticipate something else entirely?"

I twisted my hands in a gesture of confusion.

"Do you think she wanted all of this discovered?" I asked him.

"Maybe this was meant only for you. And her."

"Does this change anything for you? Does it look familiar?" Pappi asked , his voice echoing through the space.

The tower was a place that should have held memories, but instead, it highlighted the void where those memories should be. I took the brushes and paints from the floor below, where the huge yellow eye stared at me.

"Let me draw your eyes, Pappi." I said. "But come and tell me what to draw. I don't want to look at them."

He came right behind me and whispered in my ear. I'd already drawn the circle at the only available spot on the wall.

"Do the pupillary ruff. That's the pearl of the eye. Mine is not entirely smooth; it has bumps, and on the right side, the bumps are slightly more rugged."

He waited for me.

"Smudge it just a bit.

"Now take the light blue and white colors; and use the yellow. Imagine thousands of light blue cilia. Those are the little lines that make the color. And among them yellow strokes. Just like that. I also have a spot like a small mole. It's on the right side. A little higher." And I drew his eye, guided by the eye that remembered itself. I wanted to experience what she had, move in her movements. Imitate her.

I wondered if I imitated her when I was little. Just a two-year-old baby. She would have been six. I probably did everything she did. Held my dress like her, made a face she'd make, ate like she did. Put my hand on my cheek like she did.

"You have it." And I did. One eye next to mine. His. The style was different and of course, worse. Her trained hand was obviously superior. Maybe I stood next to her sometimes, while she painted.

"Would you wait for me in the car?" I asked Pappi. "Sorry for being an asshole."

He walked out. The door swung shut, gently, like it had closed itself.

The room had been waiting for this. For me. And I wanted to spend some more time with her alone. See something only meant for my eyes.

I climbed the ladder, one rung at a time. At the top, I ran my hand over the hatch and pushed. White flecks of chipped paint rained down. I pushed harder, and it gave.

Head first, I pulled myself over the cylinder, scanning the space around me. Colors swirled, shifting in the dim light—patterns I couldn't quite piece together at first.

And I saw it then.

From the outside, the whole damn roof was an eye. A perfect iris in a perfect circle. Selen's iris, staring and unblinking at the sky. Ever-watching. Everlasting. Trapped between being and not being. And once I saw it, I couldn't unsee it.

The colors were still striking, even under layers of dirt, leaves, and time. Whatever the hell she painted with, it wasn't cheap. It wasn't going anywhere. Like she wanted it to outlast everything—even herself.

Still on the ladder, balanced on the last step, I rose halfway through the hatch and ran my fingers over the metal outside, pressing and groping. My nails scraped against something rigid. A small bump. What was it? A cloth? A tape? I lifted myself up to see it better. Layers and layers of black electrical tape I couldn't scratch out. It was water-resistant and, it seemed, human-resistant.

I had to come down and take one of my sister's dummy knives. When I came back up, I started cutting through the tape. I knew there was something in it. I started feeling it as I cut through the layers. And finally, I found her secret. I held it in my palm. She had hidden it. Now it was mine. A key.

It was one of those small, old keys—the kind that opened basement doors. Its red tag felt brittle between my fingers, the faint scrawl—No. 49—smudged, half-erased by time. There was nothing remarkable about it, and yet it felt heavy, like it had carried so much.

"Look what I found," I told Pappi, victorious, dangling the key as I walked to the car.

Pappi reached for the back door, but I caught his wrist. "Sit up front."

He sighed, then he gave in.

We drove side by side, watching the fields roll by, quiet settling between us. And for a moment, I felt something like happiness.

"I have a riddle for you," I told him.

Pappi turned his head, just enough to show he was listening.

"Which would you prefer?" I asked. "Having a key but not knowing which door it opens? Or facing a door with no key to unlock it?"

Pappi squinted at the road ahead, like he was really considering it. "I'd prefer to have the key."

"But how would you find the door it unlocks?"

"That's the whole point," he said. "You'd have to go looking." Then he glanced at me. "It beats standing in front of a door you'll never open."

"The thing is, Pappi, I want to find Selen. And I will."

He didn't answer right away, just sat there, staring at me like he was trying to decide if I was joking, or crazy, or both.

"You said you're looking for something," I went on. "Help me find her. Go down this road with me." My voice cracked but I kept going. If I could just sound confident enough, maybe he'd believe me. Maybe I'd believe me.

Pappi let out a sharp breath. "Ayla—when I came to see you today, I thought this was a catch-up. A light meeting between friends."

"And?" I asked.

"And," he parroted. "Now I see it's not just a catch-up. It's an investigation. One we have no business running."

"It's not an investigation. It's a quest. In St. Luke's, we talked about *On the Road*, remember?" I cut in. "Your favorite part, the one that hit you hardest, was Dean. You said that. How untamed he was, the pursuit of the unattainable, forever chasing after a father he'd never catch."

He ran a hand through his hair. "That was just talk."

"Bullshit. You meant it."

"And what if I did?" he shot back. "That doesn't mean I'm looking to dive headfirst into some mess. Books are books, Ayla. Real life's got consequences."

I laughed, sharp and bitter. "You literally said you want to live in a cave, for fuck's sake. And this is too crazy for you?"

His jaw tensed. "That's different."

"How?"

Silence.

I leaned in. "Well, here it is, Pappi. The road. I'm offering you one. And I don't give a damn if it makes sense—I have to take it! And I know you feel it too. You've been waiting for an excuse to go."

"And what if we don't find her?"

"Then we keep moving." I held his gaze. "Or at least we find something worth finding."

"Let me think about it," he said after a pause.

And then he laughed, this loud, full-throated laugh that startled me.

"I knew you were busted up," he said. "But I didn't know you'd gone mental. And why do you avoid talking to the police?"

"The police are banking on me for answers, " I said. "They don't know shit so they are asking me. But I don't remember a damn thing. Laskaris says I might never remember her, and that's not necessarily a bad thing. Her words, not mine. I don't even know if she's a good psychologist."

I exhaled, pressing my fingers to my temple. "Maybe it will come to me when I see her. They think I am pretending. Sometimes, many times, I don't even know if I'm pretending. I'm always pretending. I don't know if what I remember is real. But one thing I know for sure? I don't remember any girl or woman named Selen. And this is all so bizarre, so unusual, that it drives me crazy."

Pappi leaned back against the seat, watching me carefully, the way you watch a stray dog—like you're not sure if it'll bite or just whimper.

"Have you talked to your parents about any of this? Do they let you stray like this?" he asked finally.

"The question isn't who's going to let me," I said. "It's who's going to stop me."

I added, almost as an afterthought, "My parents don't know a thing about me. The same might've been true for her. I don't believe them. I don't want them. I don't trust them. Not because they're liars, although they are, but because their illusions about me are so grand. And maybe the same was true for her—Selena, Selen, Seli. Whoever she is.

"You said you wanted to start living like a hermit," I said, after another long pause. "Help me deal with this mess first. You want purpose? Maybe me dragging you into mine is a coincidence. Maybe it isn't. Then you can disappear off the face of the Earth, if that's still what you want."

We drove back to town in silence, neither of us speaking.

"Let's go out tonight," I said as he prepared to leave.

He shook his head, barely more than a movement. "Not tonight. I'm wiped," he said and got out of the beat-up Opel.

10: CRIME AND PUNISHMENT

On the way back to the college, I stopped to get gas. The tank was nearly empty, and the car was coughing like it was about to die. I still felt weirdly euphoric from what we'd found in the tower. Did I think my sister was alive? The thought of her being dead wasn't as devastating as I thought it should've been, which made me feel guilty. Guilt was always there for me, hanging on like an uninvited guest you couldn't quite get rid of.

I handed the cashier a crumpled bill, my mind already on what more to say to Pappi, when a hand landed on my shoulder.

More than a friendly touch—this was a possessive grip, firm and meant to stop me.

Shit. Shit. Shit. If I was caught driving, my whole court deal could go to the shitter.

It was him. The young detective who rarely spoke. No uniform, but definitely cop vibes. How did he even find me? Did he follow me? Did he follow us to the tower? My heart felt like it was trying to climb out of my chest and into my throat.

"Getting gas, are we?" he said, casually, like we were old friends catching up at a coffee shop.

"My friend is," I said too quickly. My voice sounded weirdly high-pitched, like I was doing an impression of myself. "I'm just paying."

"Oh? Where is your friend?"

"She's in the bathroom," I said, trying to sound casual. "I'm just settling the bill."

He nodded, like he was buying it, and for a second I thought maybe this wouldn't be the disaster it so obviously was.

"Mind if I wait with you?"

Mind? Did I *mind*? My thoughts were a void. I shrugged, pretending it didn't bother me, even though my whole body was screaming, *This is it. This is how I go to prison.*

The detective—Makris, that was his name—was tall, tall in a way that made him seem extra cop-like and he was clearly about to ruin my life.

"Officer," I said, trying to redirect the conversation.

"Makris," he corrected me, his voice calm, like we were having a polite disagreement about coffee orders.

"Yes, I remember your name," I said, trying to recover.

He nodded. "So, where's your friend?"

"She ate something," I said, touching my tummy, the words tumbling out too fast again. "Something bad. She's in the bathroom. I'll go check on her."

"No need," he said like he had all the time in the world. "I'll wait with you."

I glanced toward the bathroom, willing someone—*anyone*—to come out so I could maybe drag them into this mess with me.

"Well, I don't know how long she'll be," I said.

"That's fine," he said.

"Don't you have better things to do than wait on girls at gas stations?" I added, trying to needle him, but his expression didn't change.

"Come with me to *your* car," he said, ignoring my question completely. "Drive it out of the way, Miss Sahin. I saw you pull off the road."

Well, what were the goddamn odds?

"Were you following me?" I asked, my voice too loud now.

"Not at all," he said, calm as ever. "A happy coincidence."

Yeah, happiness itself.

"Why don't you just let me go?" I said, my voice breaking a little at the end. "Let's talk about this."

He walked me outside, his hand firm at my elbow. I moved mine to the lot, then lingered for a moment before slipping into the passenger seat of his blue sedan. The interior smelled faintly of leather and cigarette smoke. He started the engine, the low hum vibrating through the floor, and the doors locked with a soft click that felt heavier than it should have. I buckled my seatbelt, the strap stiff against my chest, while he adjusted the rearview mirror with practiced ease.

He was holding my life in his hands, at least that was my impression then, but he also didn't call anyone. He didn't talk to any of his police friends or the other detective, and he was off duty. Something was happening, but I wasn't let in on the plan.

"Where are we going?"

"I'm taking you to the place where you belong."

"What place is that?"

"Prison."

That man was not taking me to prison. He was bluffing. Was I being stupid, getting into the car with him? Absolutely! My legs were bare and I had a skirt on that suddenly felt painfully short. I didn't want to be here.

He touched my leg.

"Don't look so scared?"

"I am."

"Of what?"

"Of you. Were you following me the whole time?"

He pulled the car over to the side of an empty street, the tires crunching on gravel. There were no passing cars, no passersby. The only sound came from the faint hum of the engine as the car settled into silence.

"I just want to touch you," he said. His voice was coaxing, almost affectionate. "You look like you need it."

Of course. Same old story. I stared ahead through the windshield, pretending I didn't hear him.

He leaned closer, his breath hot against my neck. His hand moved onto my thigh, heavy and deliberate, and slid up under my skirt.

"Relax," he murmured. "It'll feel good. You'll see."

I didn't want this. I didn't *need* this. My whole body was stiff, frozen in place, but he didn't seem to notice—or maybe he didn't care. His hand moved higher, fingers brushing against my underwear, drawing slow circles like he was testing the fabric, testing *me*.

"Come on, I saw how you were looking at me." he said, his tone harder now, impatient. "Help me out here. Be my good girl."

I turned my head to look at him, and for a second, I thought about saying something—anything—but the words wouldn't come.

"Come on," he said again, louder this time. "Do I have to say it? You know what I want."

He pulled back, reaching for his belt. The metallic *clink* of the buckle was the loudest sound in the world. Then the zipper, the fabric shifting.

"No," I said finally, my voice barely more than a whisper.

"What?"

"No," I said again, louder this time.

He laughed—a sharp, humorless sound.

"Oh, you'll do it," he said. "You will. Otherwise, I'm taking you in."

I shook my head, but my body didn't move. He reached for my hair, grabbing a fistful of it and pulling hard enough to make my scalp sting.

"You want me to let you go?" he said. "Then convince me right now. Do that and you're free to fly away, little bird." His hand lifted slightly, fingers tilting up in a mocking imitation of a bird taking flight.

I tried to push him away, but he didn't budge. He pulled harder, yanking my head toward him. My hands flew up instinctively, but he caught my wrist with his free hand and shoved it down.

"Stop," I said, panicking now, my voice cracking. "Please, just—"

But his grip on my hair tightened, and the rest of the sentence dissolved in my throat.

"You're going to do this," he said, his voice low and tight, like he was straining to keep it calm. He licked my lips. "Don't make it harder than it has to be."

He kissed me and then his hand guided my head down, pressing it into his lap. I wanted to fight, but I didn't. My mouth opened. Whatever, Ayla. It's just a blowjob. It won't be my first. It won't be my last. It won't be the end of the world either. I've sucked off men far uglier than him. The mission was more important. Staying out of prison was more important.

It happened in moments. Disconnected, jumbled moments. The sound of him breathing, heavy and uneven. The smell of him, sweat mixed with deodorant. The taste, salty and metallic, making me gag. He moaned and then he finished in my mouth.

The fleeting allure I once glimpsed in him had rotted into something ugly.

"Good girl," he said, and I wanted to die. Would he at least stop calling me a *good girl*? He was getting off on it. I wanted to make him come, just as a precaution against actual fucking.

He let go of my hair and leaned back in the seat, breathing hard. "See?" he said. "That wasn't so bad, was it?"

The back of my hand dragged across my mouth, wiping away saliva. I couldn't look at him. My face burned. I fumbled for the door handle and stumbled out of the car, hoping he wouldn't come after me. The hot air hit my face like a slap.

He hit the gas and was gone, leaving me standing in some alley in Thermi.

I ran into the first café I saw and reached for the toilet. But I held a little secret. I still had his sperm in my mouth. *Don't swallow. Don't swallow. Don't swallow for fuck's sake.* I sat on the toilet seat with my phone clenched in my hand. I didn't even realize I was shaking until I tried to type in Google, *"how long dna evidence lasts."*

My fingers fumbled, hitting the wrong keys over and over. It took three tries before I could string the words together. The results popped up immediately, lines of text that blurred together as I scrolled.

DNA evidence can last decades if stored properly.

Okay.

Keep cool and dry. Use a freezer if possible. Avoid contamination.

I read those sentences over and over, my breath catching in my chest. My mind wasn't processing it as fast as I needed it to. Cool and dry. Avoid contamination.

I pulled a sanitary pad out of my purse, and unwrapped the pad. That was not going to work. I typed another search:

"how to preserve saliva and semen dna"

I skimmed the answers:

Use an airtight container.

Plastic bags should work short-term but aren't ideal.

Refrigeration or freezing is best for preservation.

My breath hitched. I stepped out of the café and ran to where Google maps directed me. This could work. Thessaloniki had a pharmacy every ten meters. I always thought that was so ridiculous, but now I thanked the Gods for it. I showed the pharmacist a photo of a sterile container and pointed toward it, then touched my throat, silently signaling that it hurt too much to speak. He understood me. I handed him some coins and stormed off.

In the back of the alley, I ripped off the wrapper and unscrewed the cap. My hand trembled as I brought it to my face, hesitating for a moment. And then I finally spat. Disgust and release mixed together homogeneously, just like the sperm had mixed with my saliva.

I sealed the container tightly and stared at it in my hands. Fuck, holding sperm in my mouth for five minutes was probably the hardest thing I've ever done in my life. And I must add, the most disgusting. It was stupid. All of this was stupid. What was I even going to do with this? For now I was going to shove it into the back of my freezer. I was done with those fucking men.

What had happened to my life? How had I gotten here? Why was I constantly in a shit situation, one after the other, as if the universe had me on some cosmic wheel of humiliation and pain, spinning me faster and faster until I was about to fly off?

The sterile container was in my bag now, sealed tight. A terrible secret I couldn't let go of. My chest felt hollow. I had been scooped out and left empty, a husk, while the rest of the world carried on.

A dog walked past me, led by a man comically small for the beast he was handling. The thing was so big it looked like a bear had wandered out of the woods and decided to play house pet; its black fur rippled like spilled oil under the streetlights, and for a second, I stopped walking because, hell, you didn't see something like that every day. But I'd seen such a dog before. A Newfoundland. Was it here to save me again?

I was at the seaside, a tiny village in Chalkidiki, with my parents and two other families, all the kids the same age as me. There were six of us in total, chaotic and loud, buzzing with the manic energy of childhood. The beach wasn't sand but rocks, slippery and warm underfoot, and I loved it more than any sandy beach in the world.

The days there felt endless, infinite. My two boy-friends and I (still clean at that age, still innocent and giggly) spent every hour of the day jumping from the rocks into the sea. Over and over. Like maniacs. We threw ourselves off the rocks like we were weightless, like nothing could hurt us.

And then there was Amon Ra. I was fascinated by that name. That Newfoundland. Huge, black, with fur so thick and shiny it looked like it could repel the sea itself. Amon Ra had belonged to someone—maybe the owner of the beach bar, maybe no one at all. He was one of those dogs that seemed to belong to everyone and no one, like he had just wandered out of the sea one day and stayed. Every time I jumped off the rocks, Amon Ra would leap in after me. Not once did he hesitate. He'd throw himself into the water with this unshakable faith, this certainty that I needed him. I'd hit the water, and before I could even turn my head, he was there. Swimming toward me, his fur slick and wet, his big black eyes locked on mine. And when he reached me, he'd stop and turn, offering me his back. His body was solid, strong, and I'd cling to him, resting my arms on his back while he floated, patient, waiting. His warmth radiated through the cold seawater, making me feel protected in a way I didn't understand at the time but missed desperately now.

We must have done that a hundred times a day. And he never failed me. Not once.

"Be careful with your ears. Stop jumping. Water might get in," my mother would call to me from the shore, her voice muffled by the wind and the waves. I didn't listen. Of course I didn't listen. Why would I? I was in heaven. I had Amon Ra. No matter how many times I threw myself into the water, he'd be there to catch me.

I fished for a pen in my bag, found one, and wrote on my palm: Amon Ra. The name looked strange in my handwriting written on my skin, too angular, too defined. But it was there. Real.

He had never failed me. He'd never let me drown.

Back at the dorms, I shoved the container deep into the freezer, hiding it in the back. Then I went to the bathroom, where I scrubbed my tongue raw; gargled mouthwash again and again, until my throat burned. I collapsed onto the bed, shaking, and my phone beeped then.

I picked it up, and it was Pappi. *"I'll help you find her,"* he said.

The next morning, as I hurried down the dormitory stairs two at a time, I saw a room numbered 49.

I stopped so fast I nearly tripped. The number was brass and shiny, just a little crooked. I reached into my bag and my fingers curled around the key with its red tag. My talisman. My breadcrumb.

Before I knew it, I was at the door. The key in my hand, the red tag swaying, as if Selen herself whispered: *Try it. Try it.*

I pressed the key into the lock. It didn't fit.

But I just stood there, holding it, as if I could will the key into reshaping itself or the lock to soften and open for me. My pulse pounded in my ears; a hot, painful pressure behind my eyes. My hand tightened around the key until it hurt. Behind me, someone cleared their throat.

I turned, startled, to see a student standing a few steps below. He had a grocery bag in one hand, his keys dangling from the other. His expression was careful, curious.

"Wrong room," I muttered before he could ask, and I pulled the key out fast.

I started skipping classes. Not all at once. First, it was just a lecture here, a tutorial there. It wasn't even deliberate; I just... *forgot*. Forgot to show up. Forgot the readings. Forgot what the hell I was even doing at the college in the first place. Professors emailed; other students emailed. "Everything okay?" "We haven't seen you in a while." I answered at first. *Sick. Family emergency. Just busy.* The excuses sounded plausible, almost boring. And then I stopped replying altogether.

I'd walk for hours instead. Around campus, through streets I didn't know, past apartment buildings, public lockers, offices. Looking. Waiting for the number 49 to appear.

Once, I was in the middle of a conversation—some guy I barely knew, who had caught me at a café and decided to flirt. I nodded, said *uh-huh* at the right moments, but my eyes drifted over his shoulder, toward the street outside.

And then I saw it. A door across the road. Gold-plated numbers above it: 49.

"Hold my spot," I said, cutting the guy off mid-sentence.

I bolted across the street, dodging a cyclist who yelled something angry at me, and stood in front of the door. The key was in my hand before I even thought about it.

I shoved the key into the lock, but it stuck. Twisted. Tried again.

It didn't fit.

I stood there for a long moment, staring at the lock. My chest felt tight, like someone was pressing a hand against my ribs, hard enough to hurt but not enough to break anything. My fingers tightened around the key, pressing so hard that the teeth dug into my palm, like I was trying to turn my hand into the lock itself.

Doors, locks, numbers. I always held the key in my hand now, ready to try it. Always the same questions in my head: *Where are you, Selen? Where have you been? Where have you gone?*

Because if I wasn't looking for her, then what else was I supposed to do?

Pappi came to my dorm one morning. The place was hollowed out with my roommates off at class. I stood at the bathroom sink, splashing water onto my face, dragging my fingers over my skin like I could scrub something invisible away. His eyes were on me as he leaned against the wall, silent and watchful. The mirror stared back; a thin fracture slicing my reflection—and his—in half.

He was holding Selen's key—my key—between his fingers. I wanted to tell him about the cop. Even about the failed one-night stand that happened right where we were standing. Instead, I stayed silent. I scrubbed at my face with a cotton pad, then patted rich serum onto my skin.

"Did you see that Netflix documentary about that cult guy?" I asked him.

"Which one?"

"The Church of Something Something Jesus Christ."

He hesitated. A flicker of recognition. "I think I know which one you mean. But haven't watched it."

"The one who has like hundred wives and fucks twelve-year-old girls and calls it *a connection to God*."

"Ah. *Keep It Sweet*, right? The Fundamentalist Church of Jesus Christ of Latter-Day Saints."

"What a mouthful. Yeah, that's the one," I said. "So what's the difference, do you think? Between him and us? He thinks he's divine when he's ejaculating into young girls. And we also often think we're divine when we *make love*. When we orgasm. When we love. When we tell ourselves it's some higher connection. The only difference is the context. Our morals tinting his deed in dark colors."

He thought for a moment.

Pappi was a person who never said *I don't know*. He always had an answer. But it wasn't the rambling tirade of a pseudo-intellectual. His words were few, but they always landed just right.

"The difference," he said, "is the disturbance he creates. For him, it is connecting him to God. To his God. And maybe it is. But for her, he is creating Hell.

"That's why," he added, "sitting on a rock by yourself... there's nothing to steal, nothing to break... It doesn't leave scars. That's the reason I want to live in a cave."

He exhaled, staring at nothing in particular. The air between us felt heavier, like we'd wandered too deep into something neither of us could pull back from.

"If Selen is dead," I asked, "do you think it matters to the universe?"

"To the universe?" He shook his head. "No. To us, it does."

"And do you think being found dead is better than not being found at all?"

Eventually, Pappi said, "Maybe you're lucky you don't remember her. And all the pain that comes with her."

"I don't feel anything."

"Then why do this? Why go on?"

"Do you think my subconscious could lead me to her?" I asked him. "Make me choose the right clues. Was that what brought me to the water tower?"

"Maybe," Pappi said. " But at the same time, I want to say, don't get your hopes up."

"Why?"

"Because reality's thick. Hard to punch through." He paused. "But also, yes. I do think we're more than our bodies," he added.

"Are we?"

"I think so."

"What are we, then?"

Maybe it was the silence that followed, or the way he uttered those three words—I think so—that felt like unshakable proof. Of the soul existing. Of us, as living, breathing things, being connected to the universe at large.

"I picture it as three shadows moving as one—the body we live in, the mind that wanders, and the quiet presence watching it all."

"The body is the wrapping?" I asked.

"A shroud, a suit," he said. "And beneath it, we're a spool of thin, unseen threads. Tied to the people we've met. The places we've left behind."

"How far do the threads go?"

"Infinitely."

I smiled at that. "The universe saying, 'I am the universe wearing a human disguise.'"

When our conversations turned like this, they always pulled me under, deeper, into some dark, warm place that felt alive.

"Come with me. I want to show you something," I said and brought him to the college's lush green forest.

"You have to be very careful with how you speak to the police, Ayla," my father said on the phone. "You are not in a position to refuse."

Only if he knew.

"Also, they might ask you questions that will help the investigation. Can't you pull yourself together, please, and go?"

Yes. Some real game-changing questions, I'm sure. Like *What do you remember from that night?* and *How did you like sucking me off?*

"I would if I could." It wasn't exactly a lie—just like saying I was sick hadn't been. I *had* been sick. Just not in the way he thought.

"I'm just worried that's you being you," he said. "One of your tricks. I'll send the driver for you. Man up and go. Take some Ibuprofen and pull yourself together."

"Would it be better if I make them sick and they don't look for her during their sick leave?"

"Don't even try it with me, little girl. You will go."

And so, I obeyed.

The driver dropped me off, but I didn't go in immediately. I went to the building on the other side of the street. I tried the door but it was locked. Still, I saw what I was looking for, a PO box 49.

I tried the key. No luck.

Thank God, only the older policeman was at the station and not the young one whose taste still lingered in my mouth, if I thought about him too much. Two weeks had passed, the reminder of it in my freezer. I wished it were his chopped head, but unfortunately only his frozen sperm.

The chubby police officer looked so utterly incapable I almost felt sorry for him. He got up. The ass on that man! For a second I wondered if he was like Levi. Someone pretending, camouflaging himself as impotent. But I would be truly surprised if that was the case. As always there was a never-ending testimony, which the police wrote down and then read out loud to confirm. *Who did I hang with? Who gave me the drugs? Had I found out who she was dating?* Wasn't that your job, dimwit?

On my way out, a hand grabbed my jacket, yanking me off balance. I lurched, stepping onto my bad leg. Pain sizzled up my knee, sharp and electric.

"When will I see you?"

His voice was low but firm, the kind that didn't expect to be ignored. His grip, tight and possessive, burned through the fabric. I couldn't believe he was doing this here, at the station, in front of everyone. His touch was strong and arrogant, a brief display of ownership.

I looked up at him. His bulk, the tense set of his jaw, the way his chest barely moved with his breath. For a second, I saw him somewhere else: at the gym, pushing hard, alone, drenched in sweat, lame in his need to prove something.

"You think here's the best place for this question?" I said, glancing around, scanning the station. Faces moved past us, uninterested, but the tension in my chest refused to ease.

"Let's go for a coffee then."

"Are you fucking crazy? I don't want to ever see you in my life again."

"In the car, you were hot for me."

"Listen," I told him. "Leave me be. You touch me and I'll fucking sing. You got that?"

And I pulled my arm away and left.

11: TWEEDLEDUM AND TWEEDLEDEE

I told my parents I had a few days off from school and wanted to come home. They sounded surprised. I knew my father owned some facilities around the city, but I had to catch him with his guard down to get him to talk to me. So, I decided to go home for a few days and try to extract the information, no matter how painful it would be for me to .

Maybe for a second I thought about speaking to my parents. To the police. Tell them about the key. But after what happened, the police were my enemy. *Relax*, Makris had whispered. Like it was for my own good.

My parents kept telling me Selen was probably dead, like that was supposed to shock me into remembering her. Like

I was holding out on them. And I had tried. God, I had tried. I had smiled when they asked me to, and answered their stupid questions about what I was doing with my life.

Why didn't I feel anything for them?

I saw them. My father, pretending to be a rock, but his silence was heavier than words. His face was carefully arranged into something solid, respectable, a man holding the world and his family together. But I saw the cracks. The way he rubbed his temples when he thought no one was looking. The way his shoulders sagged under the weight of something unspeakable, something he would never say aloud. The way he had started losing things—his keys, his glasses, his sense of direction—small but significant things. And my mother. It had been a while since she last washed her hair.

And yet. Nothing.

I saw their suffering. I recognized it, labeled it, studied it like a scientist pressing a slide under a microscope. And still, there was only the dull, hard place inside me, the part that did not yield.

What was wrong with me?

Other people felt things for their parents. They wept for them, raged for them, loved them with a deep and terrible urgency. But I could not. Even as I watched them unravel, I could not.

I thought, perhaps, that I should. I thought, perhaps, that one day I would. But today, there was only this.

And the mission. The only thing that mattered. Maybe Selen wasn't dead. Maybe she was out there somewhere, waiting for me to find her. Or rotting in someone's dungeon. I wanted to find her either way.

I looked at the key again. I didn't know what I was going to find once I unlocked whatever door it was meant to open. Maybe it would be her. Maybe it would be her body. Maybe it would be nothing at all, and I would finally fall apart for good. But I had to try. I had to. Because the alternative was sitting in one place, waiting for the world to come at me. And the only time it came was to crush me.

The hole in my head didn't shrink. But I didn't care. All I cared about was her. I would do it myself. With Pappi. Even if it killed me. Especially if it killed me. Because what else was there?

The riddle that constantly played in my head. A jingle that said, *where's the key from?* I fished in my mind every second of every hour.

"Ayla, do you want breakfast?"

Where was the key from?

"No, Mother."

"Sit here with us anyway."

"Ayla, did you brush your teeth, Missy? I felt your toothbrush and it wasn't wet."

What door did it open?

"You inspected my toothbrush?"

"Ayla, would you stop being lazy and help?"

"Can't you just let me be, Mother?"

Where was the key from?

My mother was the worst—not in the way some mothers are the worst, not cruel or drunk or hysterical, just absent in a way that made her absence feel like a presence, something heavy pressing down on you. I knew she was on antidepressants. You could see it in the way her eyes didn't quite focus, the way she nodded at the wrong moments.

I thought if I talked to my mother about boys, she might react. Mothers talk to their daughters about boys. I thought it would be something she would respond to, no matter how much I personally didn't need it.

"I feel good, Mom. Don't worry about me," I lied. "I'm doing better in school. Looking forward to graduation and everything."

"You've always had it in you, Ayla," she said. "To be a leader. Since you were little. Remember your dance classes?"

"Dance classes? Really, Mom?"

"You were so pretty. You had such a sense of movement. Elegance." She smiled faintly, almost like she meant it. "Then your father had to enroll you in that manly sport."

"Basketball?" I shrugged. "I liked basketball. It gave me something to do, made me popular. School sucked, but basketball helped."

"Helped you with the boys," she said, her smile twisting.

"Not only with the boys, Mom. But yeah, sure."

"Maybe we were too loose with you and your sister," she said, and her eyes started to well up. "Maybe we should've held you tighter."

"You can't stop teenagers from having fun."

"Oh, your sister was so beautiful." That was the ultimate praise my mother gave. There was nothing above *beautiful*. I didn't know if that was meant to strike me, but my empty look provoked her to say something in her defense. "I mean you were the charmer, the tomboy. I blame basketball. But she was fragile, delicate, elegant."

"So she had boyfriends?" I asked, parroting the police. I hated that question, but it slipped out anyway.

"I don't think so. Your sister was... the epitome of a good girl," she said, but I didn't believe her. My mother wasn't in touch with reality. None of us were.

"And me?" I asked.

"You always had to be noticed," she said. "You couldn't walk into a room without making sure every man saw you. Family or strangers, it made no difference. You needed their eyes on you. Their attention was something you couldn't live without. That's what mattered most to you."

"The way you say it sounds like it's a bad thing."

She stayed quiet.

"Can a kid be bad?" I asked, but did not wait for an answer. "Anyway, I have Pappi now, and he is so many things to me."

"Pappi, your physiotherapist from the hospital?" she asked again and again, every time I brought him up. I didn't know why it seemed so impossible to her.

"Yes, Mom."

"That is so bizarre."

"And who were Selen's friends?" I asked casually. My mom had to be tricked into telling me things that were important to me. Like *I love you, Let me hold you, You're a good girl.*

"There were those two, always with her. I thought they were brother and sister, but no. Not really. The ones with the same names. Teo and Teo. Theona and whatever the boy's name was."

Teo and Teo.

I didn't answer right away. A name is nothing, I thought. A sound. A shape in your mouth. But this one came back to me as if from a distance, faint and unclear, like hearing a song you almost remembered but not quite. Teo and Teo. A tickle at the back of the throat. An ache in the chest. A shadow cast where no shadow belonged.

"Do you remember now?" she asked, and at the first moment, I didn't realize what she meant. I rolled my eyes at her.

"No, Mother. I still don't remember Selen. You'd be the first to know if I do, I swear."

A million-dollar question: Were my parents happy I was spared that emotion, or did they want to include me in their pain? I am sure my mother craved the latter.

Anna knew where both Teos hung out. The beach and the sea were a strange magnet for many of us. I still didn't know where the appeal came from. What was it? Evolution clawing its way up from the deep? Something old and slippery in our minds, a piece of us still amphibian? *Stay close*, it said. *Stay near.*

I watched out for Teo and Teo. It wasn't difficult to recognize them. They were the only people on the beach who fit the right age, though something about them seemed worn. Had Selen's disappearance left them like this? The girl sat folded into herself, her knees drawn close, her shoulders hunched. Her hair was brittle and pale, with dark streaks near the scalp that spoke of neglect or defiance. The boy had that feral thinness of a stray animal that had survived too many winters. But not unattractive, just beat up. His mouth tightened when he spoke, but his eyes—dark and endless—stayed on me, watching for something, though I didn't know what. Was their relationship brother and sister-like? Were they lovers? He was a seven. But he could also be a six or an eight, depending on the kind of day he had.

"It's so strange you don't remember her," the girl said finally, her voice level but prodding, as though testing me. "That you're talking about her and there's no emotion. Aren't you panicking? Gutted?"

"There is an emotion, but it's the wrong one," I shared. "There's nothing in the place of sorrow, only a shadow of it. Like the way you see a very young person's grave, but someone you didn't know. And you feel intensely bad for them for a second, but it quickly fades away."

The girl took a breath, like she was steadying herself, and started talking. "We told the police everything," she said. "We told them that you'd know. That you knew her better than anyone. You both were always together. She was secretive with us about men and relationships, and all that, but not with you."

I didn't tell them. Couldn't tell them about my own project. My notes, the scraps, the pulling apart of what was left. Chasing her shadow, chasing her blood. The "most probably dead" thought that followed me everywhere, while they sat here waiting. I asked instead, "Was she like me?"

Teo rubbed her hands together. "She wasn't like you," she said. "Not with guys. If she ever acted that way, we figured it was because she was following your lead."

"To keep up with me?" I asked.

Her voice was harsh, dripping with something close to disgust. "You hit on her boyfriends. You didn't care who they were or what it did to her. You went to parties you shouldn't have, left with guys who weren't worth shit—too nasty, too dumb to remember your name the next day. You ran away from home, over and over, and she followed you like a fool, every time. She was the one who pulled you back when things went bad. But this was your thing, wasn't it? You two against the world, making messes and calling it freedom. You liked trouble. Both of you did."

Trouble. The word stayed in my mouth, bitter, heavy. I thought of Selen climbing into my bed in the middle of the night. Her weight pulling the mattress, her breath too close. Whispering things I can't remember now. Something from nothing. Nothing from something. Did it matter? Maybe it mattered.

"Tell me a story," I said. "Something about her and me. Something you can't forget."

The guy started, slow and halting, like he was climbing the memory as much as telling it.

"We were in the backyard behind your house," he said. "Near the shed, there's this old tree with the low-hanging branches—the one we used to climb when we were kids. You went for it. You didn't even say anything, just started climbing, fast like a squirrel. Only you weren't a squirrel. You were drunk. Your legs were slipping but you didn't care. You didn't even stop to look down. And Selen was watching you. Remember?"

No. But I didn't want to interrupt him.

"She didn't shout at you or try to stop you. She just waited a second, like she was figuring something out, then, slowly, she went after you. She tested every branch first, gripping tight like she didn't trust it. You never looked down, didn't even notice her. But she was right behind you. We thought you'd fall. Thought you'd break your necks, both of you. But you climbed to the top and sat there. She followed and sat beside you. You stayed up there for what felt like hours. I don't know what you said to each other.

"Your parents came outside, calling for you. They didn't see you right away. They saw us first. And then they spotted you both at the top of the tree, laughing like it was all a joke. You spat down, and your loogie almost hit your mother. We were all shocked at how bold you were, how disrespectful. Your mom got so angry, she looked like she might climb the tree herself just to drag you down."

We all went quiet for a second. I didn't know what to say. I looked at the girl, and she took a breath, shifting her weight like she didn't want to speak, but then she did. "It was that party. Just a couple months before you crashed and she went missing. The one at the house up on the hill. Remember?"

I didn't.

"Selen came in wearing a dress. Your white dress."

"You froze when you saw her. I don't think you said anything at first. Just stood there, watching her walk through the room like she owned it. And she did. Everyone was looking at her. Even you. You kept nagging at her about it all night—*Why'd you take it? You didn't even ask me!*—and she just laughed, tossed her hair, told you to relax. Said it wasn't a big deal. But I could see it in your face. The way it got to you.

"You were following her around the party, drinking too much, watching the way people looked at her. Watching a guy you wanted looking at her. The dude had been circling you but not that night. Not after she walked in wearing your dress.

"She was laughing with him, leaning into him, like she didn't even notice you standing there. And maybe she didn't. Or maybe she did, and she wanted to play with you. Either way, you walked away. Out to the balcony, by yourself, with a drink in your hand and that look on your face. Like you hated her.

"When you came back inside, she was still there with him. You didn't say anything, but you waited until she wasn't looking. I saw you. I don't know if anyone else did. You took the drink from the guy's hand, something red, and poured it all over her dress. Which was your dress. The room went quiet. We all stared.

"But Selen didn't shout. Didn't even flinch. She just looked at you. Really looked at you. Then she laughed—louder than the music, louder than anything—and walked out of the room. And that was it."

I needed a minute to imagine the scene Teo just described. But her image was still absent. Not there. And it was so damn close, within arm's reach. And I reached. But nothing.

"Do you know if we or she had some place where we hid things maybe? Some place other than home that was at our disposal, at her disposal?"

They thought about it for a second and shrugged. It stirred no memories. I thanked them.

Teo walked me home. He said he had one more story, if I wanted it, and I nodded.

"It was late at night and Selen said she wanted to go to the sea. The four of us walked down to the beach. It was empty. Just us and the sound of the waves. She was the first to run in. She stripped down to her underwear and dove straight into the water. You stayed on the sand, watching her. She shouted back at you, *'Come on! Don't leave me here!'* She was laughing. So you kicked off your shoes and walked slowly into the water. Not like her—all at once, but step by step. Up to your knees, your hips, your shoulders." As he spoke, his hand traced the movement over his own body—knees, hips, chest—like he didn't notice he was doing it.

"She swam out past the buoys. You followed. The two of you were like otters, splashing each other, playing in the dark. She floated on her back, staring at the stars. You stopped too, treading water. You were far out now. Too far. From where we stood, we couldn't hear what you were saying.

"She said something, and you froze. Then she went under. Just like that. One second she was there, and then she wasn't. I thought she was joking. Messing with you. But she didn't come back up. Not for ten seconds. Not for twenty. And you dove under. You were looking for her. You came up gasping for air, and dove under again. She wasn't there.

"You started shouting then. Screaming her name. We started taking off our clothes to come look. And then suddenly—there she was. She emerged, maybe ten meters away from you. Calm. Too calm. I'll never forget the look on your face. Like you didn't know if you wanted to scream at her or swim away from her.

"You swam back to shore first. She stayed out there longer, watching the waves, watching us. When she finally came back out, she didn't say a word. Just sat on the sand, soaked and quiet, staring at the sea. You didn't speak to her either. None of us did. We just sat there, waiting for something, though none of us knew what.

"I think you two were always daring each other," he said, his voice low, like he really wanted an answer. But I couldn't give him one.

We said goodbye, and he kissed my cheek—warm and lingering, like it meant more than it should have.

I was swimming in a sea of someone else's emotions. And that sea was sticky and treacly, and it called to me. But I wasn't ready to submerge. I wanted to complete things. I wanted to change context, but in order to do that, I had to solve the current reality.

Pappi and I made a list of all public spaces that required a locker and could have the number 49. We checked local bus and train stations, gym lockers, the public pool's lockers. No success. But it was fun to spend time together. It was a fresh breath of air. To have an agenda, to have precise places to go, people passing by and the opportunity to discuss them, joke about them. Now and then, the fun would fade, replaced by something else—a quiet suspicion, a sense that every stranger might hold a clue. That every stranger might be involved in Selen's disappearance.

When I came home one night, my father was sitting at the table. My mother had fallen asleep in her chair. The house was dark save for the single bulb burning in the kitchen. He had made me an omelet. It sat on a chipped plate before me, the steam curling up and disappearing into the gloom. My father was now slicing bread, the knife moving steadily through the crust. I sat at the table, spinning my glass of water between my fingers, watching him.

"You're using the wrong knife," I said.

He paused and looked down at the knife in his hand, then at the uneven slices he'd made. "Works fine for me."

"It's tearing the bread," I said, smiling faintly. "Mom would lose it if she saw this."

I took a bite out of the omelet. It was good. Simple. Better than I expected.

"It's strange you're cooking for me," I said.

He didn't look at me. "Why is that?"

"I don't think you've ever done it before. Have you?"

"These are women things," he said. "This and sandwiches. That's my repertoire."

"Shouldn't people know how to feed themselves? A little more than just cutting and slapping bread together?"

"That's why I made the omelet."

I poked at the edge of it with my fork. "You've got spaghetti in you too, I'm sure. That's man food."

"Can't go giving away all my tricks at once." He almost smiled—but my father never smiled. Not even at his own jokes. (Which made them funnier sometimes.)

He was quiet for a moment. His hand rested on the edge of the table.

Then, as if the question had just occurred to him, he asked, "Where are you spending all your time?"

"Doing research," I said.

"For what."

"A project for university. An article. I'm trying to graduate. Move on."

He looked at me then. His face hollow in the dim light. "Why?"

"I can't stay here forever."

We sat in silence. The ticking of the clock filled the room, steady as the passage of years.

"Isn't that what you want?" I asked. "The bird leaving the nest and all that?"

He rubbed a hand over his jaw. "It'll be hard for your mother if you leave too."

I looked at him. His words hung there, heavy, like something pulled from deep within him.

I leaned back in my chair, watching him. The shadows shifted as he turned his gaze toward the window. The dark outside pressed against the glass.

"Your sister," he said. "She's like you. Always in her head. Never thinks about consequences. That's where your mother and I failed. We weren't hard enough on either of you."

I stared at him. "She's run off before?"

"She has."

"And?"

"We found her. In that old shipping container down at the docks in Kalochori." He paused, looking past me. "She stole the key from me."

My heart kicked against my chest, and for a second, I thought he could hear it too. When I spoke, my voice was flat, held together with nothing but willpower. "What happened to it?"

"We sold it."

"To whom?"

"Someone answered the ad," he said, shrugging.

"That's the first I'm hearing of it."

He looked at me then, his eyes shadowed. "Why would I discuss it with you?"

"Why do parents always think sharing things with their kids is such a bad idea?" I asked. My voice had an edge, and I didn't care if he noticed.

"Because you don't work," he said. "Because you don't take responsibility for anything. Every kindness is punished. Do you want me to go on?"

"Go ahead," I said. "It's what you're good at. Talking about how bad I am. Like Mom does. Oh, wait—no. She doesn't talk about anything anymore."

His jaw tightened. "Don't."

"She doesn't even come out of her room unless she has to," I said. The words came quicker now. "She's just lying in there, taking pills, staring at the ceiling. It's like she's already gone, isn't it?"

"Stop it," he said, but his voice wavered.

"She doesn't care about you. Or me. She doesn't care about anything anymore. And you just let her rot in there, because it's easier than dealing with her. That's what you're good at. Leaving things to rot. What probably Selen is doing right now."

It happened so fast, I didn't see it coming. A smack across my face, hard and clean, the sound bouncing off the walls. My head jerked sideways, my cheek on fire.

I didn't say anything. I didn't look at him. My mind was already in that container. The dark corners of it. The things it might hold.

I pushed the plate away and stood. My chair scraped the floor, loud and jarring. I left without a word, without looking back, and went into my room.

It was dark, narrow, and lonely.

12: THE CRYING OF LOT 49

Pappi was caught up in his own story, painting diagrams of his new journey as a hermit or whatever exactly he was going to do. He always did that when he had to figure something out, like drawing shapes was the key to unlocking the universe. I never got it. Just get on with it, man. What are the circles for?

I figured maybe it was fear. Fear of slipping from this life completely, disappearing into whatever hole he thought was waiting for him. I didn't think he'd actually go through with it. People talk big when they're planning their exit. Most don't have the guts to pull it off.

But then again, I didn't know him like that. Not really. Pappi was still a stranger to me in a lot of ways, and at the same time, I didn't think there was another person that currently knew me better than him. He had a harsh way about him. An ant-like discipline, grinding away at something no one else could see.

We met at this boho café, the kind where no piece of furniture matched. A sagging couch sat next to a chair that looked stolen from a flea market, and the tables wobbled if you leaned on them the wrong way. The walls were cluttered with crap—old band posters, paintings of God knows what, and shelves full of dusty books no one would ever read. The place smelled like burnt coffee and incense, like it couldn't decide if it wanted to wake you up or put you to sleep. He saw I was in pain and didn't hesitate; he just sat me down on the couch and started massaging my bad leg the way he did back at the hospital. His hands moved with that same professional precision, squeezing the tight, tortured muscles, finding the knots and working them loose. I barely flinched—I was used to it by now. The way he'd grab my leg in strange places, rotating it this way and that, his voice calm as he told me to try a particular stretch, a specific movement. It was clinical. But it was also something else. Care.

"I know what the key is for," I said. "I'm so sure, it's crazy. You want to go? My father might tell the police, if I'd given him the idea. Maybe he already has."

He didn't say anything.

"Will you come with me?" I asked.

"Are you scared?"

"No," I said.

He looked at me like he didn't believe it.

"Why do you want me to come?" he asked.

"It's our quest," I said. "We're in this together, aren't we?"

"You could do it alone. Wouldn't it matter more if you did it yourself?"

"I'm alone enough as it is," I said. "I want to do it, I do. I just don't think I can do it by myself."

He looked at me for a long time. Then he nodded.

"Alright," he said. "Let's go."

The shipping containers sprawled in uneven stacks, a mix of the beaten and the pristine. Some stood defiantly bright—red, blue, green—fresh paint unscarred by time; their steel sides gleaming like they had just rolled off a distant ship. Others, battered and worn, bore the weight of their history; rust streaking down in jagged lines, graffiti curling in chaotic loops, doors hanging open to reveal shadows deeper than they should have been. They leaned into each other like secrets passed in the dark. Beneath them, the cracked concrete ran on, littered with weeds and shards of broken glass, though here and there the sun caught flashes of order—containers, locked and labeled, waiting for their next voyage. The air carried the sharp tang of salt and oil, and the occasional clang of a crane punctuated the restless hum of trucks. It was a place balanced between purpose and neglect, where some containers held promise and others only memory.

The numbers were easy to track and follow, but the last shipping container from the row was 48. No fucking way. But then Pappi spoke.

"Hey, Ayla, what's your favorite number?"

And I saw it then, a little secluded, a lot bigger than the other containers, a lone and yellow little house, numbered 49.

The key fit—rusty, a little off, but damn it, it worked. The doors of the shipping container swung outward with a heavy groan, as if resisting.

And inside—God, inside—nothing like what they expected. A room, too neat, too lived-in. A room out of a dollhouse, set in place and left untouched. A TV, dark and silent. Books lined up in a careful row. A tiny wardrobe door left slightly open. A small table. And on the couch, shirts tossed carelessly, waiting for someone to return.

"Do you think it's her hiding place?" Pappi asked.

"I don't know," I said. "But wouldn't I remember it if she brought me here? Wouldn't it feel familiar, even if I couldn't place her in it?"

"It's possible. Amnesia can do a lot of things," Pappi said.

"Can you check outside? Keep watch?" I asked. "The police might be onto this place."

Pappi nodded and left. As soon as he was gone, I pulled a tissue from my pocket and began flipping through some books on the shelf, careful not to leave fingerprints. I wasn't sure what I was looking for—something small, a thread to pull; anything that might explain what this place was to her. But the more I searched, the more the questions multiplied. Did she live here? Or was it just somewhere she came to disappear?

On the edge of the table, there was a brass lighter engraved with initials I didn't recognize. My fingers hovered over it before slipping it into my pocket without a second thought. Just beside it, a pack of playing cards. That, too, vanished into my pocket, smooth and fast.

A small silk scarf lay on the arm of the couch, folded but carelessly so, like it had been worn and forgotten. I ran my fingers over it, wondering if it was hers, if she'd left it here intentionally.

I moved to a stack of papers, flipping through them with the tissue still pinched in my hand. Receipts mostly. Useless. Then one caught my eye, a date circled in red: **31.12.22, 18:45**. Of course. I pocketed that too.

The room felt smaller suddenly, suffocating with questions I couldn't answer. I stood there for a moment, the tissue crumpled in my hand.

I kept my search light, avoiding anything that would leave traces, but I couldn't stop myself from poking around. A *War and Peace* edition caught my eye—it looked out of place among the rest of the stuff. I picked it up, flipped it open. The pages had been gutted, hollowed out. Instinctively, I felt sorry for the book. But lo and behold, someone had hidden a stash there.

My breath caught.

Inside was a paper bag, wrapped tightly in brown tape. On top of it was a white label with a number scribbled on top: eight. I could feel the weight of the bag and knew what it was even before I fully processed it. Something sandy, maybe coke or heroin.

And as it sometimes happened in life, someone spoke behind me.

"Who the hell are you?" the man said, and fear gripped me. He looked at the book I was still holding.

The man had yellow eyes. I knew those eyes. Yes—those eyes from the water tower. The big yellow eye on the first floor, standing alone, watching. That color was unmistakable, extraordinary, like a cat's eyes catching light just right, a kind of glow that both attracts and warns.

"I'm not here for that," I said, lifting the book just enough for him to see. Then, slowly and deliberately, I set it down on the nearest surface. "I don't care about it at all."

"I don't know you," he said. "So, I'm asking again, who the hell are you and what are you doing in my place?"

Okay, so this was his place.

"I am just looking for my sister, and I think you know each other. Selen."

The way my sister had drawn his eyes, I knew there was something between them. I couldn't say what it was; I hoped he was not her kidnapper or her killer. Where the fuck was Pappi? He was some shit lookout.

The man didn't seem to know me. Maybe we had never met. But, at least, he should have known *of* me. Why had she hidden him from me?

"Let's put it this way. I know you two knew each other, but I don't know any details. I was in an accident the same night she disappeared. I just want to know what happened to her. If she's alive. But I'm not after justice or whatever you might be thinking. I haven't talked to anyone. No one even knows I'm here. Maybe you don't care. Maybe you do. But I'm still saying it."

Theona had said I had a thing for my sister's men. Not an accusation. A fact. Selen's first love, she said, was Dimitris. I remembered him, but not as hers. I remembered him as mine. I was a teenager, wild for him the way you get when you've decided something is love, and nothing could convince you otherwise. But Teo had said he was Selen's first—not her first lover, her first love. My infatuation matched the year they had been together. He was a heroin user. Not strung out. Not skeletal. But regular. I knew that. Selen left him, Teo had said, and it cost her everything. Years later, here I was, all grown up. Decided on taking. That was the word I used now: decided. It didn't feel like a decision then. I remembered the press of his body, his breath, his hands under my clothes like they belonged there. Park benches, dark corners, his fingers rubbing me through my jeans. I wanted him. All of him.

Until I didn't.

At his place, we were supposed to finally do the deed, but I couldn't go through with it. I made up a lie—something about a vaginal infection. Something stupid and embarrassing. He just nodded, like I'd handed him a piece of truth, which, of course, was a lie.

After that, I disappeared. I stopped answering his calls. But he didn't stop calling—first from his phone, then from others. Did I stop the affair because of Selen? Because of what she'd been through with him? Was it loyalty? Twisted loyalty, because I shouldn't have dipped my fingers in the barrel of honey to begin with? But the sweetness was there, irresistible, glistening in the light, and I knew it wasn't mine.

Right now, as I was standing in this ridiculous container, I found the man in front of me irresistible too.

"You were together, weren't you?" I asked Yellow Eyes. My voice was low, steady, though inside, something trembled. As I spoke, I caught sight of Pappi standing just beyond the door of the container, his frame half hidden by the narrow entrance. He gestured for me to stay quiet. I obeyed without thinking, shifting my gaze back to Yellow Eyes, pretending not to notice anything at all.

We all stood there silent. All three of us marinated together in the white noise of the sea.

"You should go now," he said, his voice so steady, so eerily calm, that it almost didn't register as a threat.

Then he moved forward. A step, maybe two. As if he was giving me time to react but also knowing I wouldn't. The air in the space changed.

"Leave, and don't come back," he said.

His shoulders squared. A tightening of muscle beneath skin. "Don't look for her. There's nothing to find here. You won't find answers."

Behind him, Pappi was creeping a little closer, noiseless, like a shadow against the wall. Yellow Eyes hadn't turned yet. He stood planted, muscles drawn tight like wires beneath skin. The room seemed to shrink around us, the heat pressing down, suffocating. "You make your peace with that," Yellow Eyes said. "If the police come here, that'll be the end of you. Get it?"

I opened my mouth to protest, but he raised his hand, silencing me.

"You've got a nice place to live, I bet. Healthy parents. Wealthy," he said with a wink. "People you love. People you care about." He paused, and it didn't sound like kindness. It sounded like a threat. "Stick to that."

"I want to know," I said.

"Maybe you do. But what's better? For both of you to get lost? Or for you to keep living your life, comfortable as it is? Because you might not get to keep it. Think about that."

I didn't let the silence linger between us. If I didn't keep him in our conversation, he'd see Pappi. His eyes would shift just a little, and that would be enough. I couldn't let that happen.

"Just tell me," I said. "Did you care about her? Did she ever talk about me? Did she ever say my name? I need to know. Is she alive? Or...?"

I continued, "That's her scarf, isn't it?" as I pulled it out of my pocket.

He looked at it with surprise, like it took him a few seconds to register the item. My voice felt dry in my throat, but

I couldn't stop. "I need to know. That's all. Just one thing. Tell me one thing." The desperation in my voice was so palpable, it poured on top of my words like gravy.

Yellow Eyes snatched the scarf out of my hand.

"I'll tell you one thing," he said, his voice quieter now, almost tender, but not quite. "She called you that night." He stopped, his gaze sliding past me, like the memory was painful for him. "She told you... 'I love you.' She told you this on the phone. She said her goodbyes. I suggest you do the same."

I trembled because of the way he said *I love you*, and because of what his words meant.

Pappi stood in the far corner, just by the door, too large to be this silent. How did he manage to stay unnoticed? I had no idea. He didn't move, but I thought he was ready to jump if he needed to. I thought Yellow Eyes was ready too, his body tense, shoulders tight, like he was waiting for a signal. Were things bound to get violent?

I stepped between them, cutting through the charged space, forcing Yellow Eyes to turn.

He was like a predator adjusting to a new angle of attack. Now the collision was unavoidable.

"We're leaving," I said, my voice even, though everything in me braced. I didn't touch him; I didn't dare. I just brushed the air around him.

His gaze stayed on me, fixed, like he was working something out. "What the...?" he asked dumbly.

I decided to take advantage of the moment, turned to Pappi, and grabbed his hand. It was there—solid and warm.

My fingers locked around his, and I pulled him toward me. "Let's go, please. Fast."

Yellow Eyes's face twitched, confusion breaking across his features. He looked from me to the corner, just for a moment, like something had slipped out of place.

I didn't look back. We threw him off, and I wasn't about to waste the head start. I ran with everything I had, and Pappi ran with me, his breath clipped. Our feet hit the ground in unison, pounding to a rhythm older than memory, older than thought.

"Should I go to the police?" I gasped, my breath tearing out of me like it didn't belong. The adrenaline was still high from running, but mostly from leaving unscathed.

"That's your call," Pappi said, his voice calm but taut like a bowstring. "But if it were me, I would."

No. The police were carrion birds, circling over corpses, feeding off the remains. Pappi didn't know. But I'd seen enough.

I pulled a crumpled piece of paper from my pocket and held it up to Pappi like a prize. "Guess what this is."

He looked at me, his face a mix of weariness and something I didn't want to name. And in that moment, I felt the sharp edge of fear. Fear that he'd leave. That he'd step back and let me spiral. I didn't know how to make him stay. Didn't even know if I should.

"It's a receipt," I said. "From Yellow Eyes's place. From a hotel I know. Out on the edge of nowhere."

Pappi's gaze stayed steady. "And?"

"And it matters. Look at the date." I turned the paper over in my hands, the edges damp with sweat. "This place... Everyone knows the things that happen out there. I know too." The roadside cut through the land, which sprawled wild and unbroken. The wildness of it was in contrast with the cheap hotel. I've seen wild horses running through it. And I've seen men too—the kind that don't belong anywhere except in the shadows, secluded, doing things they don't want seen.

"What things?" Pappi asked.

"Drugs, prostitutes, take your pick."

"You think they have something to do with your sister?"

I nodded, the air between us heavy with unspoken truths. "Maybe she threatened them. I'm still groping in the dark though. And Yellow Eyes... I think he cared for her, in some warped way. But he's not going to help us."

Pappi exhaled slowly, the sound like the creak of an old door. "So now what?"

"I'm going to follow this," I said, holding up the receipt again. "Even if it leads me straight into the jaws of whatever's out there."

"Or," Pappi said, his voice steady, his eyes locked on mine, "you could go to the police."

I laughed, short and bitter. "No. This is mine, Pappi. Mine to dig up. You heard him," I continued. "He said she called me." My voice was almost detached, like I was reporting something that had happened to someone else. "The night it happened. He didn't say it outright, but I knew what he meant. She said goodbye, Pappi. She said, 'I love you.' That's what he told me. She was saying goodbye."

Pappi's silence was cutting into me.

"She's dead," I said, the words harder now, louder. "That's what he was trying to tell me. She's not missing. She's gone."

I stopped to breathe, but it felt like the air in the car had thinned. "I don't remember her, Pappi. I've spent all this time looking for her, piecing together fragments, and now... now I find out she's dead. And I don't remember her."

I swallowed hard, my throat raw. "I should've known her. I should've loved her, and I can't even remember her voice."

Pappi pulled me in. A quiet, urgent motion. His arms locked around me, and I could feel his jaw set against my hair. He smelled like the forest.

"You don't know that for sure," he said, his voice nearly lost in my hair.

"I don't," I snapped, my voice shaking but firm. "That's why I'm going."

The silence that followed was unbearable. It pressed down on me, heavy and suffocating. This wasn't just a quest for my sister anymore—it never had been. It was a quest for a ghost.

"It isn't over then?" he asked me. "That's not enough for you?"

"No."

13: SLAUGHTERHOUSE FIVE

I was doing my due diligence that day, right before it all went to the shitter. Played the good girl. Gave blood. Pissed in the cup. *Piss clean*, or else. The yellow-urine leash the police kept on me—twice a month now, because I'd been so goddamn consistent. Consistently pissing clean, consistently giving clean blood samples, consistently bending over for their little ritual. Biweekly humiliation, all to keep them from yanking me back into court. The cup was warm in my hand, uncomfortable, pathetic. Like the whole charade that institution proved to be.

After that, I had my appointment with Laskaris. The next day, Pappi and I would head to that roadside cheap hotel to finish what we'd started. Just him and me. Pappi and I against the world.

The hallway to Laskaris's office smelled faintly of lemon and bleach, a smell that could almost convince you things were under control. Almost. I knocked once, then pushed the door open. She looked up from her desk, a coffee cup balanced precariously on the edge. She didn't smile.

Laskaris motioned for me to sit, and I took the chair across from her, its vinyl cushion cracked and splitting, stuffing leaking out like a secret.

"What position are you in right now?" I asked her. "Are you bound by confidentiality, or do you report to the police?"

Her eyebrow lifted, a small gesture that still managed to feel monumental. "Why are you asking?" she said. "Our current conversation is confidential."

I nodded, exhaling like that was enough. Like it meant I could say anything. Except—that's not what I did.

I told her about an ex of Selen, how I'd been drawn to him, how he felt like home. About our supposed history with boys. A version of Yellow Eyes that wouldn't make her ask more questions. Wouldn't make her think about reports or investigations or police.

Then, carefully, I told her how I *imagined* Selen had called me that night. How she had said she loved me.

"Do you believe me?" I asked her. My voice cracked on the last syllable, but I didn't care. "What do you believe about me? Have I forgotten Selen? Will I never remember her?"

Laskaris tapped her pen against her notebook—once, twice, three times. "You might remember," she said finally. "But, as I've said before, you might not." She leaned in, studying me like I was something under glass.

"You know," she said, "trauma, pain... it isn't linear. It doesn't follow a straight path, A to B to C. It's messy. It's... adaptive. Your mind looks for ways to survive, and sometimes that means reshaping what happened, how it happened. Creating a scaffolding. And you, Ayla..." She stopped, her gaze sharper now. "You're very good at reshaping."

This sounded like an accusation, but I was too curious about what she had to say.

"There are three possibilities altogether, aren't there?" she continued. "First, everything is exactly as you've said. The amnesia has erased the memories of every moment you shared with her. Second, you're lying..." She hesitated, and I could feel the weight of what was coming. "Third, you've wrapped a lie around yourself so tightly that it's indistinguishable from the truth."

Her words hung in the air, heavy and impossible to avoid.

"So, the amnesia is a story?" I asked. My throat felt tight, my words small.

"A story you've told yourself too well," she said.

"What's the difference between the second and the third possibility?"

"In the second, you're in control. You're the author of the lie, holding the pen. In the third..." She leaned further forward, her voice hushed now, almost kind. "The lie is the author. And you're just the story."

I stared at her, my chest hollowing out. Maybe this was who I was now: a story that even I couldn't unravel.

Laskaris set her pen down, a small, deliberate motion that felt louder than it should have. Her eyes were on me, heavy and searching, as though she could see every piece of me I didn't want her to.

"When you've been hurt, when things get too big to carry, you lie," she said, matter-of-fact. "Not just to others, but to yourself. You fabricate—whole scenes, whole memories. It's a defense mechanism. Your mind builds a narrative, one that fits, one that protects you. And maybe this time, the lie got too tight. Too perfect."

There was a pause, like she was waiting for me to say something. I didn't.

"So the real question becomes," she said finally, "what's the difference between the first and the third option? Between the medical condition and a story you've built?"

"And?" I asked.

"It's almost nonexistent," she said. Her smile was faint, the kind you could miss if you blinked.

"So," I said, "what's the advice here?"

"We keep peeling layers off the onion."

You're wrong, I thought. *Not we. I. I keep peeling it off. Pappi and I.*

"If everything you know about yourself is just memories—every moment you've lived—and your brain authoritatively decides what to keep and what to throw away from the memory folder—then how are you supposed to trust any of it? What if it's wrong? What if the stuff it cut, the stuff you don't remember, is the stuff that actually matters? Like, who or what's making that decision?"

"Who do you think?"

"Is it me? I want to say it's me. That my brain and I are the same creature. That, ultimately, the decision maker and I are the same person. But why doesn't it feel like that? Why does it feel so… determined? Like the choice was made long before I ever had a say in it."

No answers. Just silence.

The hotel had no advertisement—it didn't need to. People found their way there anyway. It was more like a cheap roadside place than a real hotel. It also didn't try to hide its decay; it wore it like a badge of honor. Nestled just past the city's edge, the hotel seemed less built and more grown—an accidental structure that sprouted from concrete but as if nature was trying to reclaim it. The sign still clung to life, barely, with a missing letter that left it reading BYZANT_O, the gap like a missing tooth in an old, weary grin.

The parking lot was cracked and uneven. Reeds pushed their way through the asphalt to remind you that the earth had its own plans. Guests came here because it felt like the kind of place where no one would find them. The place had a way of finding the right people. People with debts to outrun, lovers to forget, or memories they couldn't bring themselves to carry anymore. A stopping station for the depressed and suicidal. It was the kind of place where you could disappear. Or maybe it was the kind of place that disappeared you. There was a gang that used that place as an office. We, the locals, always knew they were there and always considered ourselves lucky that we didn't have anything to do with them. Up until now.

Regardless, I was excited about Selen, about Pappi, about us. The three of us. I wanted to talk him out of ditching the city, out of leaving everything behind. I wondered if he was planning to ask me to go with him. But I kept my mouth shut. No point in saying anything until we found what we were looking for.

The place was damn near deserted. There were just two solitary old cars parked in front. And beyond them, a pair of massive TIR trucks loomed in the back; their hulking shapes casting long shadows across the cracked asphalt. We were going to spend the week here and if we didn't see anything, maybe I'd tell my parents about Yellow Eyes. And they could go to the police.

The 'reception' was empty when we got there. A bell sat on the counter, chipped and rusted, like it hadn't been rung in years. We stood around, waiting, calling out. Finally, a girl shuffled out from the back, wiping her hands on her jeans. She looked half-asleep. We rented a room. Nineteen euros a night. She took the cash and slapped a key on the counter. Not a word. Just turned and disappeared again.

The rooms were functional in the way a body was functional when barely alive. Our room smelled faintly of rotting vegetation. The wallpaper, once pale yellow, had long since turned a mottled brown-green, curling at the edges like it was recoiling from itself. The furniture didn't match—an armchair upholstered in cracked faux leather, a particleboard nightstand with a cigarette burn that looked like a map of the Aegean.

It was so ridiculously unkept, Pappi and I just looked at it and shook our heads. Classic. Just classic.

Brownish water gurgled in the pipes, and the television picked up two channels, one of which was static.

The first day passed in a strange, almost feverish haze. We dragged two chairs to the window, our makeshift watchtower. The curtains hung crooked, pulled just enough to let us see out without being seen. That was the plan: to watch, to wait. To see if someone suspicious showed up. To observe the gang I knew hovered here—their movements, their dealings. Maybe even take a wild guess at the truth about what Selen had gotten herself into.

We stocked up; beers lined up on the chipped table, junk food spilling out of plastic bags. I set the binoculars and my laptop on the windowsill, the screen glowing faintly in the dim light. We had movies—plenty of them. Each of us picked a favorite. The air turned stale quickly. Outside, the world stayed quiet; the parking lot blurred by heat and distance. And still, we waited.

"You brought binoculars?" Pappi laughed, shaking his head.

"Of course. What kind of stakeout would it be without them? You didn't?"

I was amazed by how that man never once got up to piss or shit. Not once. How the hell did he hold it? What did he do—wait for me to leave for the bathroom and slip outside to relieve himself like a dog on a tree? The thought stuck with me, circled my brain like a fly I couldn't swat. It made me painfully aware of my own body; the heaviness in my bladder, the dull ache in my gut, like I was the only one here chained to the basic, humiliating needs of being human.

"You think anyone will show up today?" I asked, breaking the silence.

Pappi was leaning back in the chair, one boot balanced on the edge of the windowsill, his face unreadable.

"They might," he said finally. "Patience, Ayla." His tone was flat, disinterested.

I pulled out the cards I had snatched from Yellow Eyes' place and held them up. "Pappi, teach me to play poker." I had asked him, just like Dean asked Sal in *On the Road* to teach him about Nietzsche.

He looked at the cards, then at me. Sighed. "You ever played?"

I shook my head.

Yeah, I'd played before. A little. Didn't matter. I wanted to hear it from him, see how he did it. People told you a lot when they thought you didn't know shit.

"But I kind of know—a flush is strong, pairs are good, two kings, two queens. And... what's it called when the cards are in order?"

"Straight," Pappi said.

"Alright," he continued. "First thing—you don't play every hand. Patience, here's that word again. And that's half the game."

He shuffled the deck, the cards snapping together in a way that made it clear he'd done this a thousand times. He dealt. "Texas Hold 'Em. Make the best hand using five cards."

I picked up my cards. "I want to know about bluffing."

He smirked. "Bluffing's what gets you killed if you don't know how to do it right."

I studied the cards in my hands, the weight of them. "Well," I said, "I better learn fast."

Pappi leaned back, tipping his chair on two legs. "You gotta sell it. Make them believe what you want them to believe."

I frowned. "How do I do that?"

He let the chair drop forward and reached for his beer. "Pay attention. Watch how the cards fall. If the board shows high cards, you act like you've got a monster hand. If it's low and messy, you sell the scrap. But if you don't believe it, neither will they."

I turned my cards over, considering. "So, it's not just lying. It's reading people."

His mouth quirked up. "Now you're getting it."

We played hand after hand, time slipping away with the shuffling of cards, the clink of beer bottles, the scrape of Pappi's chair against the floor.

The bed was too small for two people. That much was obvious the moment we saw it—barely a full size, with a sagging middle and a thin, scratchy blanket thrown on top. It was the kind of bed designed for function, not comfort, let alone intimacy. Neither of us said anything when it became clear we'd be sleeping in the same bed. I sat down first and the springs groaned under even my slight weight. By the time we gave up watching the window, in the early hours of the morning, the air between us had grown too thick to argue over details, and we were ready to collapse into the dirty pillows.

The mattress smelled faintly of mildew, the damp, sour scent rising as though it had been waiting for the warmth of a body to release it. I lay down on one side, stiff as a corpse, facing the wall. Behind me, I heard Pappi hesitate, his footsteps slowing, a pause so long I thought he might take the chair or the floor instead.

But then the mattress dipped again, heavier this time, and the smallness of the bed became a suffocating fact. His warmth and the quiet rustle of his breath made my skin prickle with a strange mix of awareness. I folded my arms tightly across my chest, pulling myself inward as much as possible, as if to say, *I am here, and you are there, and this is how it will stay.* But the silence pressed harder, thicker, until even my own heartbeat felt like an intrusion.

"You okay?" he asked, his voice low, almost whispering.

"Yeah," I said quickly, sharper than I intended. It wasn't true, but what else could I say? There was no language for this, for two people lying side by side, close enough to touch but careful not to.

I could feel him shift, the faint movement of his weight traveling through the mattress, and I squeezed my eyes shut, willing my body to relax. But the awkwardness sat heavy in the room, in the bed, between us. It wasn't about the space, or the lack of it—it was about everything unsaid, everything unacknowledged, hovering over us like smoke.

Eventually, his breathing slowed, evened out, the rhythm of sleep overtaking him. But I lay awake, my back to him, listening to the faint creak of the bed as it settled under his weight. The mattress sagged in the middle, pulling me toward him like a quiet inevitability. By morning, I had drifted into the sag without realizing it, my shoulder brushing his.

By the second day, we didn't care much about dressing or undressing. It was awkward at first, sure, but it faded fast.

I hadn't meant to stare, but as he pulled his shirt over his head, the way his back moved caught my attention.

"Your body's... surprisingly fit," I said finally. "You look like you could carry someone out of a fire."

"Thanks, I guess," he said, looking at me sideways. "You sound surprised."

"Not surprised. Just thinking," I said. "You've seen my body plenty of times. In the hospital, broken and taped back together. Do you think you look at bodies the way the rest of us do? Or is it different for you now? After everything you've seen? All the bodies you've touched?"

He rubbed the back of his neck; his jaw was tight, like he was deciding how much to say. "I figured out how fragile they are," he said. "That's about it. Otherwise, I guess I don't see bodies all the same. I have preferences."

"Like?"

"I like it when people maintain their bodies," he said, shrugging. "It's more about what it says—discipline, movement. But I like women's bodies that aren't so muscular. My friends, some of them are bodybuilders. They're ripped, ten percent body fat, all that. For women, though? I don't know. I like the softness. Little flaws here and there. Makes it real."

It was Pappi's choice to pick the movie today. He said the movie was good, *Eternal Sunshine of the Spotless Mind*. I'd never seen it before. "You'll like it," he said and winked at me as it began.

We watched the parking lot as much as the film, our eyes flicking to the window whenever there was movement. A man appeared first, walking slowly, his shoulders hunched under the weight of a backpack. His steps were uneven, his head bowed, as if he didn't want to be seen. He passed under the streetlight and into the shadows, gone as quickly as he'd come.

A while later, a woman crossed the lot, her coat too big, her heels piercing the asphalt. She moved fast, her head down, the *click-click-click* of her shoes inaudible from where we watched—but in my mind, I heard it. Neither of them stayed. They just passed through, their stories brushing against ours but never meeting.

The movie played on; scenes flickered across the screen—fragmented memories, erased and stitched back together. When it ended, the credits rolled in silence; the soft glow of the screen the only light in the room.

I turned to Pappi, trying to cut through the weight of the movie, of the night. "So you picked this movie for me?" I asked. "What, because it's about erasing painful memories? Very subtle."

He smirked, finally pulling his eyes from the parking lot to look at me. "Well, I figured it might be relevant," he said, playing along, his tone just dry enough.

"What do you think your life will be after you find her?" Pappi asked me. "Do you plan on chasing a career? A family?"

"I'm not a career-and-family kind of girl. You should know that by now. I'll be free," I said, the words spilling out too quickly. "No strings, no obligations, no husband's warm breath on the pillow beside me. No. I'll be wild. I'll drink until the edges blur... I'll fuck every man I meet. And I'll laugh. I'll be a fire burning everything in my path—mountains of coke, bottles of gin, hours on the dance floor, spinning and spinning and spinning until the world is gone and it's just me. Alone. And the fire."

Pappi's eyes were on me, watching closely. "You can't live like that forever, can you? No one can."

"Maybe I'll be a businesswoman for a little while. My father will be too old or dead by then, but he'd have been proud. I'll have three kids, maybe four. Four babysitters. I might be divorced, but proud of it—proud that no man can keep me. I'll have a plane ticket tucked into my purse, just in case I need to disappear. I'll be magnificent.

"Then I'll change again; I'll be a hippie. My house will smell of patchouli and weed, the floors covered in cushions, strangers singing, laughing, smoking. Like the beat generation. My children—grown by then—will not understand me. They'll mutter about me to their friends. Their crazy mother. Barefoot, distracted, always lighting candles.

"And then I'll be floating in some far-off place. Psychedelics will have burned holes in my mind. My hair will fall past my ankles, white as ash. The DMT pipe will be fused to my hand. People will come to me, asking for answers. I won't know the answers. I'll barely know myself.

"Then I'll be an artist. Not a good one—not right away. But I'll get there. I'll write books. Maybe one or two will be good, good enough that people will notice. Movies will be made. My name will float in the air like perfume. Men will want me. Women too. I'll be drunk in interviews, at awards shows. Best Thriller, 2043. Or maybe just Best Local Author. Who cares? Success will wrap itself around me like a lover, tight and suffocating. I'll take it everywhere. To dinner. To bed. To the mirror, where I'll smile at it and cry with it. And when I'm done, when I've wrung it dry, I'll move on again.

"And then—I'll be nothing. A loser. Broke. Useless. Unwanted. A shadow. Who will want me then? When I've burned through everything—through everyone?

"Someday, though, in the in-between of it all, I'll teach. My students will be my life. I'll live for their approval, their disappointment. There will be a boy who wants me. A girl who laughs at me. Most of them won't care about me at all. They'll take my class because they have to. I'll stay up all night grading their papers, reimagining their faces. Alone.

"I'll wear glasses, of course. And I'll imagine things. Things I shouldn't. A student—sweet-faced, bright-eyed—staying late, leaning in. *Miss,* he'll say, *is there anything else I can do?* One time, I will give in to the temptation. Only once, I promise."

Pappi laughed softly, the sound low and warm. "Your poor students," he said, shaking his head.

The potential of the situation was there—Pappi and I could feel it humming, faint and persistent, like a light left on in another room. But the desire? It wasn't there. Not for me. Not for him, I thought. At least not now. There was a love story somewhere between us, sure, and we told each other that story with our eyes, with our mere presence. We told it, let it loop, and stretch and break, and then we let it go. Let it drift downstream, taking all the words with it, until there was nothing left but the silence of what we'd almost been. Pappi's face was pale in the dim light, the faint glow of it stark against the dark. And I would remember that moment. I would cherish it for the rest of my life.

On the third night, I woke to the sound of the lock turning. A faint, metallic scrape, too deliberate to be a mistake. For a moment, I didn't move. My body was awake now, rigid, but my mind lagged, heavy and clouded. The door clicked open, and a pale light spilled across the floor, creeping toward the bed.

Two men entered. I could see their shadows first—long, jagged things that reached across the room like fingers. A woman followed them, her figure smaller, keys still jangling in her hand. It was the receptionist.

The blond man stepped into the room first and flicked the light on. His hair was almost white, his skin too, tattoos spidering up his throat and curling along his jaw. He didn't look at me right away. Instead, his eyes swept the room, the faintest hint of a smile curling at his lips.

"Busy night," he said, more to himself than to anyone else.

The second man moved to the edge of the room, his hand brushing over the dresser. He didn't seem to be looking for anything in particular, just touching, testing, like he was trying to see what this place was made of. Then he found the binoculars, lifted them to his eyes, and peered through with a chuckle.

And then I saw the third man.

I hadn't noticed him at first. He had been standing just outside the door, in the dark. The blond man turned toward him, gave a small gesture. *Come in.* And he stepped forward.

Yellow Eyes.

His left cheek was swollen, the purple spreading like a slow bloom beneath the skin. *What the fuck…?*

I sat up, clutching the blanket to my chest. "What the hell is this?" My voice cracked, and the blond one finally turned to me.

"That her?" the blond guy asked Yellow Eyes.

He nodded.

The blond man grinned, looking like he was about to enjoy himself. "What are you doing here, sweetheart?"

"Is it against the law to stay at a hotel?" I asked, kicking Pappi under the sheets. "What are *you* doing here?"

"Let's see. Loverboy here said you paid him a visit. And our thorough caring receptionist told us about a girl in distress, acting all strange. Alone. In a place like this." He spun in a slow pirouette, as if to present the room to an invisible audience.

"I was worried about you," he said. "It's the sort of person I am."

I glanced at Pappi again. His posture was calm, head turned toward the wall, like he wasn't in the middle of this mess. He didn't move, didn't even flinch. "Pappi—" I said, but the blond one cut me off.

"Who are you calling?" he asked, tilting his head like he was amused, like I'd said something that intrigued him. He moved away from the door and stepped into my space before I even realized he'd closed the distance. He reached out and tucked a lock of hair behind my ear, the gesture so delicate that his fingers brushed my skin in a tender caress.

I pulled at Pappi's arm again, harder this time, but he didn't budge. His body might as well have been carved from stone. "What have you done to him?"

The blond man barely glanced at me. "Did you see anyone else with her?" he asked the receptionist. Whatever she said, I missed it. My heart was pounding too loud.

"Your work here's done, baby. You can go now," the blond guy told the receptionist.

She didn't argue. Just turned her winged ass around and left.

"This'll be more fun than I expected," he said, clapping his hands once before sitting on the bed beside me. "Start talking, little girl. Who sent you? You think you can just walk in here and stick your nose in our business?"

"Your business?" I said, my voice sharper than I meant it to be. "I don't care what you do here. I told him that." I jabbed my finger at Yellow Eyes, pointing like it might burn him. "I'm looking for my sister. She's missing. That's all this is."

Yellow Eyes met my gaze. There was something there. Remorse, maybe. Or nothing at all.

"I was only trying to help," he murmured.

The blond man waved him off. "You can go now," he said. "Your friend and I need to have a little chat."

Yellow Eyes hesitated for a moment, then left without a word.

"So, what is it? What do you want from us?" the blond guy asked.

I could barely hear him over the blood pounding in my ears. My breath was hot and tight in my chest. I turned to Pappi. He was supposed to protect me. But he just lay there—completely still. Had they smothered him? Drugged him?

I started running through my options, fast.

"You need to get out of here," I said.

The blond man frowned. "Why would I do that?"

"Leave," I said, louder now, looking from one face to the next. "Before..."

"Before what?"

I stared at him, my chest tightening. "You're wrong," I said. "He'll fight you. People will hear." I jerked my chin toward Pappi.

For the first time, both men turned their heads.

The blond one looked at Pappi, then back at me. "Who do you think will help you right now?" he asked again.

My hands were shaking. "He is—" My voice broke as I turned toward Pappi, reaching for him, fingers digging into his shoulder, shaking him hard.

The blond one's words sliced through the room. "There's no one there, sweetheart. Just you."

I blinked, my breath catching, but I kept holding onto Pappi, as if his warmth would confirm he was real.

"No," I whispered. My hand hovered in the space where Pappi's body lay heavy.

The brick of a man by the window snorted.

"I know who you are," the blond man spoke, calm and conversational, and leaned in. "So the question is, do you know who I am?" His face was close. His breath smelled faintly of mint, like he'd just spit out his gum before walking in.

"If you scream," he added, putting his forehead against mine, "this will be over before it begins."

The tears were there now, hot and blurring my vision.

"Don't cry, sweetheart. You found us. That's what you wanted, isn't it?" He pulled back, as if to catch me in all my distress; like he was feeding off it. My forehead felt unclean; his skin was greasy. It felt like he'd marked me.

I'd imagined this before—this exact moment. Lying in bed at night, staring at the ceiling, picturing someone breaking into my apartment. Just as a mental exercise. Wondering how I'd protect myself. What I'd do. Would I jump out the window? Would I run for my phone and lock myself in the bathroom? Where was my phone now? But then their words came back. *There's no one there, sweetheart. Just you.*

My stomach twisted. My pulse was racing, but my brain wasn't catching up. Pappi had to be here. He *had* to be. What kind of sick fuck was this blond man? My head was foggy, like the floor under me had shifted and no one told me. Where was that damned phone?

I fumbled through the sheets, my hands trembling, the fabric bunched up beneath my fingers. The phone was here—I'd felt it earlier, hadn't I?

"You looking for something?"

I froze, my hand still buried in the folds of the blanket. I turned my head slowly, and there he was—right there, his pale eyes fixed on my face.

"Don't stop on my account," he said. "Go on. Keep looking."

My fingers tightened on the sheets, the panic rising in my chest.

"I'm not—I wasn't—"

"You weren't what?" He leaned closer again. He reached out then, slowly, deliberately, and picked up the far end corner of the blanket. "Maybe it's in here," he said, his tone soft and mocking. "Want me to help you find it?"

"No," I said quickly. Too quickly.

His arm brushed against my thigh as he fished around. Then he pulled back, holding up my phone, warm from where it had been pressed beneath Pappi's body. "Looking for this?"

He turned the phone over in his hand and, without warning, tossed it across the room.

I shook my head quickly, my mouth too dry to speak.

He just stayed there, so close I could see the fine lines around his eyes, the faint smirk pulling at the corner of his mouth.

"Keep your hands where I can see them," he said.

The words sounded like a bad movie line, something a cop would say to a guy caught robbing a liquor store. And it made me want to laugh. But there was nothing funny about this. I placed both hands in my lap, fingers curling into the blanket.

"Good," he said, his eyes flicking to my hands, then back to my face. "See? That wasn't so hard."

I couldn't keep looking at him, couldn't hold the weight of his gaze.

"You know, I don't mind helping. I'm a helpful kind of guy," he said. "But I don't like being lied to."

"The police know I'm here," I said, and my voice wavered. "They know I'm here. They'll come looking for me."

"Oh, the police?" He said it lightly, almost playfully. "They know you're here, huh?"

Then his voice dropped. "Didn't I just say I don't like being lied to?"

I had the sudden sense that I was somewhere else entirely—somewhere vast and empty, a place where sound didn't travel, where no one could hear me even if I screamed.

"They know," I said, louder now. Like a kid trying to sound tough. "I told them where I'd be."

He exchanged a glance with the Hulk-man by the window, who just snorted softly, shaking his head.

"Do you hear that, *malaka*?" the blond man said. "She told the police where she'd be. They know she's here."

The room filled with laughter, low and bitter, the kind of sound that crawled under your skin. I let it wash over me—the humiliation, the fear, the walls closing in.

Get it together. This wasn't about fear, or whatever they wanted me to feel. This was about *her*. And me. About getting answers. I could panic later, scream into a pillow, break things if I had to.

I clenched my fists and reminded myself why I was here.

"Let me tell you something," he said. "If the police know where you are, then where are they? Hmm?" He pulled back and spread his arms wide, like a showman revealing an empty stage. "Where's the cavalry? Where's your savior?"

I opened my mouth, but no sound came out.

"I'm the sister of the girl that disappeared." I recited. "Selen Sahin. Do you know where she is?"

"I know you're looking for your sister, girlie. See, the thing is..." He leaned in again, his pale eyes level with mine. "People like you? You think you've got leverage. You think you're smarter than us." His voice dropped, soft and almost kind. His hand reached forward, and before I could react, his fingers were already in my hair.

His hand moved gently, too gently, combing through the strands with a mock tenderness that made my stomach twist. But I didn't pull away. I didn't dare.

"You don't," he said simply. "You don't have leverage. You don't have power. You've got *nothing*."

I stared at him. He smiled faintly as his fingers lingered at the nape of my neck now, his thumb brushing my skin there.

"You came all this way for answers," he went on. "So I'll give you one. You want to know why people like you never find what they're looking for? Because you think you're smart," he whispered. "But you're not. You're just privileged. And privileged bitches always bleed the same."

I swallowed hard, the sound loud in my ears. My body was frozen, every muscle locked in place, but my mind was racing, screaming at me to move, to do something.

"I'm going to give you a little advice," he said, his hand grazing my cheek before falling away. "Let this go. Go home. Pretend you never came looking."

I opened my mouth, the words spilling out before I could stop them. "Where is she?"

The faint smile on his face faded, his features going blank. For a moment, he didn't say anything. Then he shook his head, like he was disappointed.

"You don't listen, do you?" He sighed. A little too theatrical. Then he stood up. "And here I was, trying to be nice. Now, I know two things you don't," he said. "Pick a hand. Left or right."

I swallowed. My heart hammered against my ribs.

"Pick."

His pale eyes locked on mine. His right hand curled into a fist. His left stayed open. Palm up. Fingers just slightly curled, as if cradling something invisible.

"Go on, pick."

"Left," I whispered, though the word barely made it out of my mouth. He smiled faintly, and held up his left hand. "This one," he said, "knows what's going to happen to you tonight."

A cold chill slid down my spine.

"And the other?" I asked.

"The other," he said, lifting his fist, "knows about your sister."

I couldn't breathe. My head spun, the implication of his words settling over me like a hand closing around my throat.

"Tell me," I demanded.

"Not now," he said, almost kindly. "Not yet. But you could find out."

"How?" I asked desperately. "How can I find out...?"

His smile deepened, a slow curve that seemed to stretch forever.

"You'll know," he said. His tone was soft, almost soothing. "If you survive everything I do to you."

The way he said it, the calmness, the certainty. It sent a shiver through me. "What if you kill me?" I whispered.

He cocked his head, as if the thought had never occurred to him. He studied me for a long moment, his pale eyes narrowing.

"I might," he said finally. "You'll have to trust me, won't you?"

"Think about it," he continued. "If finding her is all you've got left—if it's more important than any fear or pain—then you'll push through. You'll take the pain and keep moving. Simple as that."

I shook my head, my heart hammering, my hands trembling in my lap. "You're insane," I whispered.

He let out a low, humorless laugh. "Maybe. But I want to know you, girlie. Be close friends."

I opened my mouth to argue, to tell him some magic words that would get me out of this situation, but nothing came out. I felt tears sting my eyes, my throat tighten. "Please," I said. "Please, just tell me. Just tell me where she is."

For a moment, I thought I saw something almost human in his expression. Almost.

"No," he said softly. "Not yet."

My breath hitched. "I can't—"

"Yes, you can," he said, cutting me off. "You're such a nice little lady. You'd do anything, wouldn't you?"

I couldn't look at him. The words hung in the air, suffocating, and he knew it. He knew exactly what he was doing, the weight he was placing on me, and he was enjoying it.

"I'll give you one chance," he said. "Endure tonight. And tomorrow, I'll give you your answer. One way or another. Don't fight it and I will tell you everything."

"Okay."

He jumped then, quick as a cheetah, and the darkness pressed.

This was the moment I understood.

Finally.

My big moment. The one I'd earned.

All these years of rehearsals, preparing, bracing myself. Since I was thirteen—maybe younger—I'd been orbiting this inevitability, circling closer and closer, waiting for my turn. And oh, the nominations. There'd been so many.

Most likely to be pinned against a wall.

Most likely to feel the rough scrape of a stranger's hand up her skirt.

Most likely to hear, Relax, it's not a big deal, whispered into her ear by someone who wasn't going to stop.

Most likely to wake up and wonder why her clothes were on the floor and not on her.

And now? I wasn't just nominated anymore.

The Oscar went to me. Me!

I'd like to thank someone.

First, I'd like to thank God!

And then I'd like to thank the man in front of me—the one grinning, striking, and sinking into me. Thank you, I'd say. Thank you for recognizing my hard work. I couldn't have done it without you.

[The crowd cheers. The applause is deafening. Someone in the back wipes away a tear.]

And I almost laughed. Almost. But no, because this wasn't funny, was it? This wasn't the part where I got to laugh. All those other times were just warm-ups. Practice runs.

Not like now.

This wasn't dipping a toe into darkness. This was the ocean. Deep and black and endless, dragging me under, pulling me so far beneath the surface I didn't know which way was up. My lungs burned, but I couldn't scream.

And hadn't I always known this moment would come? Hadn't I always felt it hovering there, just out of reach? Just like Selen.

Pappi didn't move. He hadn't moved at all. But now he was facing me. His body was flipped toward mine, lying there like someone had rolled him over while I wasn't watching. The same position, the same dead weight, but turned toward me, like a mannequin set into place. His eyes were open. Staring into mine. The mattress rocked, shaking everything but him. His body stayed still, like it wasn't part of any of this. The room trembled, but he didn't. I stared at him, waiting for something to make sense.

Nothing did.

A moth throws itself against the glass. *Whump. Whump. Whump.*

I count the beats. One... two... three...

Flip

You like this, don't you?

He rolled me out of bed. I hit the floor hard—face first into the wooden floor. Something cracked. My head? The floor? I couldn't tell. My back arched, something snapping deep inside.

                    Flip

Boss, you'll kill her too.

I'll stop when she stops moving.

The walls tilted, and blood filled my mouth—hot, metallic, rushing over my tongue.

You think you're above this?

                    Flip

Spread fucking open, you sick, fucking stupid bitch.

I pulled like mad, and my face slammed hard against the floor again. Pain exploded through me. Blood gushed out, warm and sticky, pooling beneath my cheek.

                    Flip

The room spun. Everything spun. And then the cold press of the floor met my back again.

He was laughing as he zipped up, the sound jagged and wrong. *Thanks for that*, he said, his voice mocking. His foot caught me in the stomach, driving the air from my lungs, and I folded over myself, coughing and choking, bile and blood mixing in my throat.

The other man stepped forward then. He'd been waiting, I realized, watching from the shadows like an animal in the dark.

You think you can just come here? Think you can ask questions about whoever?

She got what she deserved.

Pain bloomed in me, sharp and electric, radiating outward in waves. I doubled over, retching, but they didn't stop. Hands shoved me, lifted me up, threw me down again. My knees hit the floor hard, the impact jarring up through my bones.

My head snapped to the side, the taste of iron flooding my mouth. I tried to crawl away with one last surge of energy, but fingers in my hair dragged me back like an animal.

The room swam around me, the air heavy with the stink of sweat and blood. I couldn't think, couldn't breathe.

Another kick, this one to my side, sent me sprawling.

So it goes.

14: WHERE THE WILD THINGS ARE

When I was a kid, pissing was easy. Hell, everything was easy. Pull your pants down, do the deed, pull them back up. No one gave a damn how it looked or where it happened or whether you got it just right. Nobody told you how your body was supposed to work; it just *did*.

Then you grew older, and suddenly there was more to it. You'd have tights to wriggle out of, jeans so tight you'd have to fight like they were trying to kill you and buttons that wouldn't cooperate. The layers piled on as you grew up, each one adding a small but noticeable hassle to something that used to be simple. You started timing bathroom breaks to fit between busy moments, rushing because someone might be waiting for you, or because you were out with friends and didn't want to be the one holding everyone up.

I was nineteen, seeing some guy. Maybe my boyfriend, maybe not. Smiling that smile, the one that meant he was up to something. "Let's try something new," he'd said. Yeah, sure. Why the hell not. It wasn't the piss itself that felt strange. It was the way I did it, crouched over him, his body warm beneath mine, his hands resting on my thighs, holding me in place. The liquid splashed onto his chest and slid down in warm, uneven streams, some of it catching in the dips of his ribs before pooling around his belly button. It felt like rebellion and dominance all at once. The apartment smelled like sex and sweat, and now piss. Afterward, I laughed, embarrassed but not ashamed.

Now, at twenty-two, public bathrooms were too loud, too crowded. The stalls too small. The floors wet. And I was always trying to balance something—my phone, my bag, my sanity. Someday I'd be old. I'd need help to do the deed. This thing I'd done since I was a newborn, something so simple, would be difficult. Slow. Awkward. Another quiet loss among so many.

Ever gotten yourself lost mid-thought? Just like that—gone. One second it was there, floating, almost solid, then *poof*. Like it never existed. It felt like a glitch. Like your brain stepped out for a smoke.

It was so utterly bizarre. But what if it was more to it? It was a special moment. I'd entertained scenarios about it.

How it could be an entrance to one of your many lives in the multiverse. You forgot your thoughts and—*bam*—you were in a parallel reality. You forgot your thoughts, and whoa—you ended up somewhere else.

It was just so fitting.

I'd forgotten my thought.

And when I opened my eyes, I realized—I'd pissed myself.

I barely opened one eye. A brown leather shoe rested next to my face, the sole cracked and dusted with dirt.

"Leave her. We fucked up with the sister already. Bad karma."

"Let her go, man. You killed the sister—that blood's on your hands already. The police won't give up so easily this time."

This was the second time someone had pleaded for me; begged for my life.

As I lay dying.

The second voice that believed I might survive. Or pretended to. The second voice hovering between mercy and indifference. The second voice that could pull me out of the grave—or push me further in, depending on who got the last word. The first one was Pappi's, and this one, I knew who it belonged to.

Pay attention now.

This was what it had all led to.

"Your sister, girlie, is buried," the blond guy said. I craned my neck, pain shooting down my spine. Just as I caught sight of him, he flicked an unlit cigarette and waved a lazy hand at Yellow Eyes. "Your friend here made sure she stayed that way."

I wanted to tell him to go to hell. I wanted to spit in his face. But before I could even twitch, his foot connected with my ribs. Hard.

Pain shot through me like a lightning bolt, so sharp I thought I'd split in half. I tried to suck in air, but all that came was the taste of blood and heat. Then the world tilted, folding itself into black.

I couldn't piece together what had happened, but I knew what I saw wasn't some trick of the light. And if it was, it was one hell of a fucked-up trick. Or maybe I was dead, and this was how hell said *Hello, Ayla. Welcome.*

"Not you," I screamed, my voice cracking like glass under pressure. "No. No. No. Not you." Spite burned through me like a jolt of electricity, pushing me upright for a moment before the pain dragged me back down.

Makris stepped closer, his face wearing the kind of pity that made me want to punch him. His hands were careful, almost reverent, as he reached for the pile of pulp that I had become.

"Don't touch me," I spat, but he was already there, kneeling beside me.

"Calm down," he said, like that would fix anything. "You're badly injured. I'm saving you." His gun hung low at his side, his fingers slack around it. In his other hand, his phone glowed, his thumb hovering like he couldn't decide who to call—an ambulance... or a priest.

He was calling for help.

I slapped the phone out of his hand. The act startled me as much as it startled him. Pain shot through me as the movement set my body aflame. My bile rose, hot and acidic.

"Get out," I screamed.

He didn't flinch. "I can't leave you like that. Please, calm down."

I grabbed onto him like I was letting him help me. He held me up like a real gentleman, steadying me. While his hands were busy, I propped myself against the bed, and that's when I made my move.

The gun slid from the holster easier than I expected, like it wanted to be held. Cold. Heavy. My thumb found the safety. A flick, a click. Years ago, in another room, another life, a man I was fucking had taught me. Guided my hands over cold metal. *Thumb here. Now it's live.*

I lifted the gun and pointed it at Makris. My wrist tensed, my fingers settled into place. My finger hovered over the trigger. I exhaled. The shaking stopped. The chaos faded. There was only this.

"If you don't leave, I'll kill myself."

I turned the barrel to my temple.

Was I serious? Was I bluffing?

Bluffing. That word. *If you bluff, make it a hand they could believe.*

But what if the bluff was real?

Makris took a step back.

"Leave," I repeated, and then I moved the gun. Pointed it at him. "No," I said. "First, I'm killing you. Then myself."

He froze. His hands hung in the air like he thought they could catch the bullet before it reached him. Idiot.

"Listen to me," I said, each word like a nail being driven into wood. "Listen fucking carefully. I kept a souvenir. Remember shoving yourself down my throat? Your sperm. My spit. I tucked it away in a freezer, waiting for the right moment."

His eyes narrowed, but he stayed quiet.

"I don't want your help. I don't want your pity. Go after the fuckers who did this to me. Go now. But touch me again, and I'll blow my brains out right in front of you. And you'll have to explain why I'm dead."

The silence was so thick it made my ears hum.

"Dumb whore," he said, finally. But he left.

I made him leave his phone. Told him if he didn't or if he called the police right now, I'd take my story to every goddamn journalist from Athens to Belgrade and I'd use my father's connections. Let them all know who he really was.

He left. He really did. I didn't think I had it in me to make anyone do a damn thing, but there he was, walking out the door. I let out a breath I didn't know I'd been holding, but it didn't feel like relief. Not yet.

I turned my head, and there he was. Pappi. Lying on the bed, facing me. His head propped on the pillow like he'd been there forever. Like he was waiting. His eyes were open. Wide. Staring at me as if I were the only thing worth seeing.

I climbed onto the bed next to him.

Something shifted deep in my gut. It wasn't fear, exactly. It was the kind of recognition that comes before fear, when you see something familiar, but it feels wrong in a way you can't explain.

But his body was there. *It was there.* His chest didn't rise. Didn't fall. No breathing. The sheets beneath him were too neat, too smooth—barely creased, like they hadn't felt the weight of him at all.

His eyes never left me.

I blinked, but he didn't. The longer I stared, the more the edges of his body seemed to blur, as if the dim light wasn't sure how to hold him. His face was calm, but not the kind of calm that brought comfort. The kind that left you hollow.

I shifted on the bed, pain shooting through my ribs, but his eyes tracked the movement. His gaze didn't break, didn't flicker.

You're not real.

My hand gripped the blanket like it might keep me grounded, but the cold weight of realization kept pressing down. His eyes weren't the eyes of someone alive. They were the eyes of something that shouldn't be here, something my mind had conjured and now couldn't let go of.

I wanted to look away, but I couldn't. My breath quickened, shallow and panicked, like my body had figured it out before my brain had. He was here—but he wasn't. He was watching me—but from where? The room around us felt suffocating, shrinking, the air heavy in my lungs. I squeezed my eyes shut. Counted to three. Opened them again.

Still there. Still watching. His eyes locked on mine. But the longer I looked, the more I felt the truth creeping in, silent and steady.

I pressed my forehead into my palms, gasping for air. His gaze burned through me, even when I wasn't looking.

I'd fallen asleep—or maybe I'd blacked out—and when I opened my eyes, there was another figure looming over me, his shadow bending into mine. Yet another man. God, I must include more women in my life. Preferably, undead women. He nudged me awake, almost tenderly, but his eyes—his eyes were so yellow, murky as moss clinging to stones. Those yellow eyes, ancient and unclean.

His hands gripped my shoulders. He pulled me up, and I felt every tendon in my body resist, every muscle scream. My legs buckled under me, and for a moment I thought I might collapse again, but he didn't let me.

"Why'd you send him away?" His voice was low, steady. Yellow Eyes fixed on me, cutting like blades.

"That's my business," I spat. My voice cracked, raw from screaming.

The corner of his mouth twitched with a ghost of a smile. Not a kind smile. Not a cruel one either. Something in between.

"I called him," he said.

I froze. "What?"

"I took your phone," he said, calm as hell, like he didn't just cross a line that made me want to punch him. "You've only got seven numbers saved. Anna. Doctor. Father. Mother. Officer One. Officer Two. Pappi."

He paused, smirking like he was proud of himself. "I went with Officer Two."

"You shouldn't have done that," I said.

He took a step back, his yellow eyes watching me, waiting. "She's in the bog," he said. "Your sister."

My head snapped up. "What did you say?"

"The blond guy," Yellow Eyes continued." He told you the truth. She's buried, but she's buried in the bog."

"What bog? And you know that how? You... brought her there?" My voice was barely a whisper.

"I did."

The room was spinning now. I swallowed hard, my throat aching. "You killed her?" I asked as a new wave of fear surged through. I couldn't take another beating. I just couldn't.

"No."

"Then how'd you know she was dead?"

"I knew."

"She could have been saved," I said, the words tearing out of me.

He hesitated, just for a second, then nodded. "She died while I was driving her to the hospital. That's when she called you."

I stared at him, my vision swimming. "Why'd you dump her body, then?"

"Dump?" He frowned, his yellow eyes narrowing. "She adored that place."

For a moment, neither of us spoke. I tried to breathe, but it felt like there wasn't enough air left.

"What happened?"

"She saw something she shouldn't have," he said. "Those guys—they were doing something. Something no one was supposed to see. And she saw it. That's why they killed her."

"Aren't you with those guys?" I asked.

The question hung there between us. He didn't answer at first. His yellow eyes shifted, as if searching for something in the room, something invisible. His jaw tightened, and the silence dragged on so long I wasn't sure he would answer at all.

"I'm not," he said, finally, his voice flat, hard. Then, softer, almost too soft to hear, "Not really."

I stared at him, the words sticking in my throat. "Not really?"

His lips pressed into a thin line. "I'm not one of them. Not the way you think. I come and go. I... fix things. Push things around for them when they need it. They trust me. But I'm not with them."

"Fix things," I said, the words bitter in my mouth. "Like what? Like her?"

His eyes flashed, sharp and hot, and then cooled just as quickly. "She was important to me," he said.

"Important." I repeated the word like it didn't make sense. It didn't. "So important you threw her in a bog."

"She mattered," he said, his voice low, insistent. "More than you know."

"Then why didn't you save her?" The question came out before I could stop it, raw and jagged.

"I tried," he said. "But there are things you don't understand. Things you don't get in the way of. Not unless you're ready to die. And even then…" He shook his head, his voice trailing off.

I felt something rise in my chest, boiling and hot, like bile or rage. "So you just let them kill her."

His expression darkened. For a moment, I thought he might hit me, or leave, or just disappear into the shadows of the room like he hadn't been there at all. But he didn't.

"I got her out of there," he said finally. "I tried to take her to the hospital. She died before we got there."

"And then the bog?" I asked.

"And then the bog." He nodded.

"Show me."

The car hummed along the empty road, the bog waiting somewhere ahead. I wondered if this was the same drive Yellow Eyes took with my sister. Only, she had been dead, which was now a subtle difference.

"Where was she sitting?" I asked him.

"Back seat."

"She died in the car? Right in this car?"

"Right where you are."

Pain twisted through my ribs, deep and liquid, spreading with each breath, each movement. I touched the seat beside me, half-expecting it to be warm, half-expecting some echo of her to still be here. The space she left behind pressed in around me—too close, yet impossibly distant.

Yellow Eyes dragged me to the container, where we first met and shoved a handful of painkillers in my palm. "The bog's right there," he said.

"Right where?"

"Come, you'll see." He cleaned the blood off my face.

I hoped he wasn't going to put me in it. I hoped he wasn't the kind of sick fuck who liked his kills in pairs. Didn't matter. There was no going back. I followed.

You'd never notice the bog. Not unless you were looking for it. And even then, it had a way of folding itself into the landscape. Hidden in plain sight. But once you saw it—once it *let* you see it—there was no unseeing it.

It was close to the container yard, close to dirt roads and power lines and on the verge of civilization, yet somehow separate. It was an area where things blurred. Where land turned to water, then back again, uncertain. A place between this world and something else. Something invasive.

The air thickened as we neared the bog. Heavy. Damp. It clung to my skin, carrying the scent of rot—not the quick, bright decay of a dead animal, but something older, deeper; the smell of earth swallowing things whole.

The bog was a wound in the land. A slow, seeping thing where colors bled together, where edges dissolved. The ground was a mottled patchwork of ochre and deep green, like the back of some vast, sleeping animal. Moss spread in thick, hungry sheets, so spongy it could swallow a foot in seconds. Its color unsettled me—that *too-bright* yellow-green, the shade of something sickly yet thriving.

The sedges swayed in the wet air with rusty tips. When the wind shifted, they shimmered, threaded with copper. Pools of still, black water dotted the landscape, their surfaces broken and uneven like old glass left too long in the elements. Overhead, the sky wavered between gray and the slow creep of morning.

"Not much farther," Yellow Eyes said, his voice low, cutting through the mist. He glanced back at me, coldly assessing, like he was studying how far I could go before I collapsed.

The ground softened beneath us, the crunch of dry earth giving way to something wetter, more insidious. My shoes squelched, then sank. The mud sucked at them, greedy, as if it knew my body was broken and was waiting for the right moment to claim me.

He moved ahead of me, quicker, lighter. He wasn't struggling the way I was. His long stride made it seem easy, like the bog wasn't dragging at him the way it was me. My feet sank deeper with each step, the mud swallowing them, the cold seeping through the sneakers and into my skin.

He stopped abruptly, just at the edge of where the earth gave way to the bog. I caught up to him, breath coming in sharp little gasps, like a dog kicked too many times. Oh wait, that was exactly what I was.

"This is where I stop," he said.

"What?" I asked, blinking at him, unsure if I had heard him correctly.

"This is as far as I go," he said again, gesturing to the waterlogged wasteland ahead. "You're on your own from here. She's somewhere in that area." And he made a circle, loose and lazy.

I looked past him. The mud oozed like a blackened wound, slick and glistening, the water shimmering faintly under the first light of the rising sun. It looked bottomless, hungry.

"You're not coming?" My voice cracked, raw from the cold and the effort.

He shook his head. "If you step wrong in the mud, it'll take you," he said simply. "It'll pull you under. It doesn't give people back." He looked at me, yellow eyes steady. "The mud decides."

I stared at him, stunned, furious, terrified. "And what if it takes me?"

He didn't flinch. "I won't risk my life. That's your decision."

I wanted to scream at him, wanted to hit him, but I didn't have the energy. He stepped back, retreating to the drier ground. "I'll wait here," he said.

I turned toward the bog, the mud glistening in the faint light. My legs were weak, my body trembling, but I forced myself forward.

The first step sank me ankle-deep. The mud was cold, viscous, clinging to my skin like it knew me. Like it recognized what I had come for. My second step sank me deeper, up to my calves now, the mud sucking at me with each movement. I pulled one foot free, the sound wet and obscene, only to sink again.

My body wasn't meant for this. My legs burned, my breath came short, my ribs screamed with every gasp.

"Keep going," I whispered to myself.

The mud rose to my knees, then higher. Every step was a decision, a gamble. I didn't know if the next one would hold or if the ground would give way entirely, pulling me under.

I thought about his words—*the mud decides*. And I couldn't stop myself from believing it. It wasn't just mud. It wasn't just water and dirt. It was something alive. I could feel it, pressing against me, pulling, shifting. Testing me.

The mud decided if I was worth saving.

I wondered if I should pray to it. Or if that would be a step too far. Yeah, right. *That* would be the step that went too far.

It pressed higher now, up to my thighs, cold and thick, weighing me down. My foot caught on something, and for a moment, I couldn't move. The mud held me there, unyielding. My chest heaved, panic rising. I tried to pull my foot free, but it didn't move. The mud tightened around me, gripping me, and for a horrible moment, I thought this was it.

It's taking me.

But then it released me. Slowly, painfully, my foot broke free, and I staggered forward.

I didn't see her. There was nothing to see. Just the endless sweep of mud, reeds swaying in the faint breeze, the surface rippling faintly like something alive.

I stood there, my legs trembling, buried to the thighs in the muck. My foot slipped as I tried to step forward, and I pitched forward, my hands plunging into the mud to catch myself. The mud surged around my arms, swallowing me to the elbows. I pulled back instinctively, but something stopped me. Something solid beneath my hands.

I froze.

My fingers brushed it again, and a wave of nausea rolled over me. It wasn't the soft, pliable muck I'd been clawing through. This was different—something hard and misshapen, coated in the wet, suffocating grime but undeniably there.

I pushed deeper, my stomach churning, my chest heaving as my fingers groped blindly through the cold, sticky depths.

And then I felt it.

A curve. A shoulder? No—more delicate. My heart slammed against my ribs as I realized what it was.

"God," I whispered, choking on the word. My breath came in broken sobs, the taste of bile rising in my throat.

I kicked my foot forward, desperate, and it struck something beneath the surface. My entire body recoiled, but my legs sank further into the mud, trapping me, forcing me to stay.

Shaking now, my fingers clawed through the layers of mud until they caught on something. It took all my strength to pull, the mud fighting me at every moment, gripping what I had found like it didn't want to let go.

Finally, the surface broke.

A hand.

Her hand.

The mud fell away in clumps, revealing skin and bone, fingers curled inward, blackened nails clawing at nothing. I couldn't breathe. My body was shaking so violently I thought I might collapse, but I kept pulling, clawing, until the mud surrendered more of her to me.

Her face came last, still somewhat preserved by the bog. I stared, transfixed by the horror of it, repelled, but unable to look away or leave.

Her hair was tangled with reeds, the mud clinging to her cheeks, her jaw, her sunken eyes. I wiped it away with trembling fingers, scraping the muck from her features until I found her, piece by piece.

The bog had eaten some of her, but it left the parts that mattered. Her face was a mess of sunken skin stretched over bone like old leather left out to dry. The nose was barely there, the mouth stuck open, the teeth dark and exposed. But it was the hair that got me—long, matted, tangled in thick, rotting knots, clinging to her skull like wet rope.

Selen's eyes were missing. Of course they were. It was only right. They found their way to the Water Tower. Because where else would they go? And I couldn't stop looking at the hair. Wet, dark, clinging to her skull like it was the last thing on her body willing to stay.

I didn't cry. Couldn't. I just stood there, breathing in the stink of the bog and the decay, and tried to feel something that made sense.

It was her.

Finally.

It was Selen.

My throat tightened. I couldn't scream. I couldn't cry. My hands shook as I reached for her hair and tore free a lock, dark and slick with mud. It stuck to my palm as I clutched it, my chest heaving, bile stinging the back of my throat.

The mud shifted beneath me, restless. Angry. It had let me find her, but I knew it was waiting, deciding whether I could leave.

I sat there, holding her hair. Not from a brush. From her. From the whole of her, dead and gone. I whispered, "I'm sorry." I kissed her then. I kissed my sister goodbye. *Did I?* Yes. And left her there.

The sunrise broke through the mist, pale gold spilling across the marsh.

Behind me, he was waiting. On solid ground. Safe. Watching. Was he, at least, real? I didn't know who made the decision, me or the mud, but I somehow, miraculously managed to wade my way out of the thick, dripping nectar of the bog.

BELOVED

"**H**ey, Ayla,"

"Selen," I said. The wheel hummed beneath my fingers, a low vibration traveling through my palms, but I wasn't really holding it. My grip was loose and lazy, the pads of my fingers brushing leather that felt slippery. "Your name—it's beautiful, you know that?" I told her. "It's elemental. Like Selenium. Something dug out of the earth. Something pure. How did I never see it before? Isn't that strange?"

She made a soft sound, like a laugh she didn't mean to let out. "Thank you for seeing me anew," she said. I could hear the smile in her voice, faint, but it was there.

"I see you all the time," I said. "Every second. Every hour. You're always there."

The sound of tires on the road was rhythmic, hypnotic. My thoughts clung to her voice as if it could anchor me.

"Are you high?" Her voice teased, lilting. Playful.

"I might as well be," I said, laughing a little. It felt good to laugh. Strange, but good. It hurt too, somewhere deep in my chest. "You make me feel that way."

Silence. Not judgmental. Just heavy. I could feel her pulling back, like someone stepping into the shade when the sun gets too bright.

"You remember how Mom used to tell us we were beautiful?" she said finally. Her voice had gone quiet. Distant. "Like it was the most important thing we could be. 'Strive for beauty,' she'd say. Like it was a goal. Like it could fix everything if we just got it right."

"Well, you're the most beautiful person I've ever seen," I said. "And not for Mom's reasons. For entirely different ones. For the opposite ones."

A long pause, her breath light on the line. "I think I was just about to say that to you," she said. My name lingered on her tongue. "Ayla."

"It doesn't matter who says it first," I said. "What matters is I love you. That's what matters."

Her smile wavered, or maybe it was her voice that wavered. I couldn't see her, but I could imagine her eyes shifting away, looking at something I couldn't see. "I love you too," she said. "But be careful, Ayla."

"Careful of what?"

"Careful not to kill yourself."

That landed. Her voice wasn't teasing now. I heard her pull in a sharp breath. "You're driving, aren't you?"

"I am."

Outside, the world blurred past—a smear of headlights, asphalt glistening from the mild Thessaloniki winter.

"Would you stop the car if I asked you?"

"Of course," I lied.

"Okay, then I'm asking."

"Selen, I love you," I said. The quiet felt like it was swallowing me whole, but I said it anyway.

"Should I believe you?" she asked. Her voice was playful, but the sadness seeped through.

"This is goodbye from me, my love," she said.

A cold gust of air through the cracked window brushed my cheek, like it was trying to wake me up. The wheel twitched beneath my fingers when I hit a bump, but I didn't tighten my grip.

Her words stayed there, hanging between us, heavy and final. She laughed after, but it wasn't a laugh. It was something wet, a sound that cracked in the middle like she was trying to hold it together and couldn't.

And then the crash.

I wished I could tell you this was a real memory. That it all came flooding back after I found her—everything. Her face. Her voice. That night. That I remembered it slowly, painlessly, as if each piece had been waiting for me to put it back together. Like peeling away old paint to find something whole and perfect underneath.

But that would be another lie. And I'd told enough of those already.

This, too, was borrowed. Stolen. Sewn together from fragments—Yellow Eyes's story about the night she disappeared. The wreckage of my crash. My own suggestions, creeping in. My imagination filling in the gaps. A half-truth. Just like always.

I kept the lock of her hair, though. Snatched it from the bog before I could change my mind. I kept it in my pocket, like a secret I wasn't ready to share. I touched it every now and then; felt the strands press into my skin, just to make sure she was real. To make sure *I* was real. That much, at least, was true.

A couple of days had passed, my wounds were too fresh for him and his stupid face, but I went to find him.

I needed to talk to Officer Makris.

"What are you doing here?" he asked.

His voice was flat, but there was an edge to it. A warning, maybe. He stood with one hand resting on his hip. He didn't expect to see me at the station, but he wasn't surprised either.

"I have three things that belong to you," I said. And my hand slipped into my pocket.

His eyes flicked to my hand, then back to my face.

"Let's swap," I said. "I know you have my phone from the crash. I know she called me. I want to hear that conversation. Can you make that happen?"

He jerked his head toward the door, gesturing for me to follow him outside. No hand on my wrist. No rough grab. He didn't touch me, and I counted that as a win. Not much of one, but I'd take it.

"That's impossible," he said. His voice was quieter now.

I smiled, sharp and mean. It felt good to let it cut.

"Here are the three things I've got," I said, locking eyes with him. "First, your gun. Second, your phone. Third, your sperm mixed with my spit."

Makris didn't respond right away. He just looked at me, his face blank, but the clenching of his jaw betrayed him. The muscle in his cheek twitched, a slow, deliberate grind of teeth, like he was chewing on the words he wanted to say but couldn't.

"Only I know where it's stashed," I added, letting the words cut through the silence. I pulled up the photo on my phone and shoved it in his face, the date and time stamped. "All that DNA. Make it happen," I said.

He just stared at me, and I stared back. I kept my hand in my pocket, fingers curled around the lock of Selen's hair.

"That's impossible," he said, finally breaking the silence. "Unless someone bugged the phones. Yours or hers. There's no way to hear it otherwise."

He sighed and rubbed his jaw, like this whole thing was just another mess he didn't have time for. "All I can do is get the call logs. Time. Duration. That's it."

"Fine," I said. Nothing more to say. I handed him back his gun, then his phone, and he took them without meeting my eyes.

Laskaris would call this progress, *Making do with what you're given*. I almost heard her voice in my head.

Call Log Report

- **Generated Date:** 2023-01-01
- **Time:** 03:03 AM - 03:16 AM
- **Duration:** 13 minutes
- **Call Type:** Incoming
- **Caller:** Selenger
- **Recipient:** Ayla Sahin
- **Status:** Completed

I went through the sliding doors of St. Luke's and asked if he was there. The receptionist looked up with tired eyes—the kind that had seen too many midnights. "Name?" she mumbled. I told her.

"Should we call him?" she asked.

"No," I said. "Don't bother."

She studied me a moment too long, as if trying to decipher what brought me here, but I gave her nothing. Outside, the day was warm and bright. I got a coffee from the vending machine and sat on a bench facing the hospital entrance, steam curling upward before fading into nothing. The coffee tasted like mud and water, but I drank it anyway. This place, right here, was the dividing line—where the real Pappi had ended, and mine had started.

The day unraveled slowly, but I stayed where I was, watching the hospital doors.

Still no Pappi.

St. Luke's towered above, a luxurious white building indifferent to everything happening inside. People went in, people came out.

It suddenly reminded me of that scene in *Patch Adams*, where Robin Williams—playing a doctor—had rigged up a massive papier-mâché pair of legs in stirrups outside the clinic door just to spite all those uptight doctors. Every poor bastard who entered had to walk straight through a giant fake vagina. Christ, I'd laughed myself stupid at that scene—laughed until the tears ran hot down my face, laughed until the world faded into a meaningless blur.

Would I ever laugh like that again?

I sighed, long and slow, like I'd been holding my breath for hours. Not hours, days. Not days—but for the whole nine months—since the accident; since I lost Selen.

Then Pappi finally came out. It was already dark and he didn't see me. He didn't even look around, just walked straight ahead, shoulders slightly hunched.

I crossed the street, fast but quiet, and tapped him on the shoulder.

He turned, blinking at me like I'd pulled him out of something. His face was blank, almost soft, but then it sharpened, and I saw the moment he placed me.

"Oh," he said. "Look who it is."

His voice was neutral, almost amused, but I heard something underneath it.

"How've you been?" I asked. Polite. Easy.

We traded words that didn't matter. Pleasantries. Small things. The fucking weather. I was healed, mostly. But every now and then, the wounds still gave a gentle jab; a kind reminder of what I'd been through.

"Pappi," I said, cutting through it. "You didn't keep your promise."

He looked at me, his head craning the slightest bit, his eyes narrow. A question.

"You promised," I continued, "that when I left the hospital, you'd give me your real name."

That made him smile—no, laugh. A small, tight sound, like something scraped out of him. "Alright, then," he said. "Why don't we go somewhere, and I'll tell you."

I smiled back.

"Let's do it," I said, as I let him lead the way.

My hand slipped into my pocket. The lock of her hair was there, rough and cold, like it still belonged to the bog. I brushed my fingers over it, over and over, feeling the weight of it.

Pappi led us past a row of shuttered shops, the windows blank and dark. No one else was around. The streetlights made long shadows, trailing and curling as we moved.

We stopped at a door marked *49*. The numbers were gold, shining dully under the dim light. The door looked like wood, but these days, you could make anything seem like anything.

"Here we are," he said, pushing it open.

And I followed him inside.

Kanina Krisalis
NECTAR. SOUNDS OF SOFT THINGS BREAKING

Editor: Haralambi Markov
Illustrator/Artist: Fabian Aerts, Emil Markov
Layout: Elena Lazarkova
Format: 148x210 mm
Print sheets: 16

Printing house Alliance Print

Printed in Dunstable, United Kingdom

68664270R20147